NEIGHBORS AND OTHER PEOPLE

Neighbors and Other People

MORE OF THE BEST OF DOUGLASS WELCH

Edited by *Ruth Welch*

Illustrations by Bob McCausland

MADRONA PUBLISHERS, INC. · SEATTLE

Printed in the United States of America

Library of Congress Cataloging in Publication Data

Welch, Douglass.
Neighbors and other people.

I. Welch, Ruth, 1905- II. Title
PZ3.W4424Ne [PS3545.E498] 813'.5'4 77-20285
ISBN 0-914842-24-2

Madrona Publishers, Inc.
113 Madrona Place East
Seattle, Washington 98112

Foreword

Douglass Welch was born in Boston and grew up in Tacoma, Washington, where his father, Charles B. Welch, was managing editor of the *Tacoma News-Tribune*. At the age of fifteen, Douglass started his newspaper career on that paper as a summertime cub reporter. After graduating from the University of Washington, he joined the editorial staff of the *Cleveland Plain Dealer*, returning to Seattle later as a reporter and feature writer for the *Seattle Times*, and subsequently for the *Seattle Post-Intelligencer*. In addition to his newspaper work, he wrote short pieces of humor for the *Saturday Evening Post*, where his "Mr. Digby" stories became a steady feature for years and were later published in book form. A number of his stories were adapted for films, radio and television, and many of his short pieces and stories were included in anthologies and collections.

After winning the Hearst Newspapers Award for humorous news reporting for two successive years, Douglass was assigned to write a daily column for King Features Syndicate, and "*The Squirrel Cage*" column was born. From the time of his death in 1968, there were many requests for a collection of his columns, and the book titled *The Squirrel Cage*, published in 1976, was the result. The very warm reception accorded that book brought forth a convincing plea for more, and this book is the result.

Editing this second volume was difficult only in narrowing the choice of material. The unconventional, individual and oblique approach to a great variety of subjects and characters that distinguishes the Welch humor tempted me to include much more. The columns finally selected are my favorites, and I hope they will be the readers'.

RUTH WELCH (Green Eyes)

Contents

NEIGHBORS AND OTHER PEOPLE

CHAPTER I

My Neighbors

I am sorry the sightseeing bus doesn't run through this neighborhood of mine during the fall and winter as well as the spring and summer. We have some fascinating sights for the adventurous tourist and, especially, for the foreigners who like to see how typical Americans live. In tourist season the drivers route their buses up my street hoping to catch a sight of The Widow, our main attraction, when she is out on her front lawn in tight pants and a clingy top working in her flower beds. The bus always slows and the driver waves and she waves back and the men tourists hang out the windows and it just kind of makes you feel good that you live in America.

Actually, the sightseeing objectives in our neighborhood are not The Widow, but the Benedict Arnold High School and Father Ryan's church down the street with the painted sign on the lawn depicting the British burning our White House in the War of 1812. The English members of Father Ryan's congregation are unhappy about his fixation against the British and they've talked to the Bishop about it, but Father Ryan, who was born and brought up in Dublin, denies that the painting of the flaming White House and its title, "Lest We Forget," is religious. He says it is fugitive art done by one of his own Sunday school seniors and, as art, it is not subject to episcopal approval.

CHARTER
TOURS
McCAUSLAND

The high school is named after a pioneer around here who gave the land and enough money for the building if they would name it after him. I remember old Ben Arnold well. On the day of the dedication, a reporter said: "You have a pretty well-known name, haven't you?" And Ben said: "Well, I should hope so. I've lived around here for forty-five years." The school's football team is called "The Traitors."

If a typical suburban neighborhood is what tourists are looking for, there should be no trouble designating one right here. The first thing that comes to mind is Mr. Dibble's mother-in-law, who sometimes stands on the front lawn in her negligee and waves at strangers in passing automobiles. She is eighty-five and drinks brandy and smokes cigars in bed. She is worth seeing. And the night tour bus could stop at the Dibbles' and go down to his basement and watch him bore holes. This is his hobby since his wife gave him an electric drill, to bore holes in plywood in the pattern of voluptuous female figures.

The bus would certainly want to stop across the street at Hixly's and see his collection of hotel soap. I believe he would pay for the privilege of showing it. And his wife, Hetty Hixly, she loves to run around in her bare feet and she paints each of her toenails a different color so that when she puts her feet together, you get a full color spectrum.

And then we have Caesar, the big, friendly St. Bernard, who sleeps in a double bed at the Peabodys' and doesn't get up until noon and mixes martinis for his master's parties. He could climb on the bus with a neck keg of martinis and his paper cups and serve the tourists, which would be a sensation.

Then we could get Mrs. McMurty, who is 40-40-40 straight up and down, to come out in her gardening clothes (her husband's old pants and an Indian sweater) and beat a dishpan to frighten the starlings off her roof. She always gives a spirited performance.

I asked my wife, Green Eyes, which neighbors the tourists might like to see and she said: "Are you planning on making our neighborhood a concession? Shame on you." And I said: "Of course not. I just thought it would be sort of hands-across-the-sea for foreign visitors to see some typical citizens, like Mr. Jack down the street whose wife gave him a cannon for Christmas." And she said: "That ought to be typical enough to satisfy anyone."

And I said: "If there were Russian tourists, we might find out why the Russians are pumping poison gas into Grandma's bedroom every night?" And she said: "Wouldn't you be ashamed of the way you talk about Grandma if you found out some day that the Russians really *have* been pumping gas into her room?"

And I said: "We could send them by the Bugle Lady's house at night when she is bugged about something and puts on her old Girl Scout uniform and steps out on her patio and plays cavalry calls on her bugle. And she said: "That would show the tourists that we Americans are not only normal, but that we are *ready*."

Come to think of it, we ought to have a neighborhood meeting with the bus company and lay out a route of all our interesting attractions. Think what we could do for International Understanding!

* * *

It has become sort of a tradition for most of the ladies' clubs in my neighborhood to meet at my house because Green Eyes has the largest coffee urn and we supply the coffee. We don't have to supply the dessert – Mrs. Blair and Mrs. Cooper generally bring the cookies and Mrs. McMurty brings the cake. But there is a rule that nobody can start eating Mrs. McMurty's cake until the business of the meeting is over.

Mrs. McMurty's cakes are monumental and women seem to lose their reason at the first bite. I mean Mrs. McMurty will make a cake fifteen inches square, three layers, dark chocolate with whipped cream and chocolate flakes and nuts between two layers and marmalade between the other.

Each time the ladies have one of these cakes they take a taste and cry out: "My heavens, this is the most wonderful thing I have ever tasted!" and then they say: "But I shouldn't!" But they do. Often there is a half or a third of the cake left over, and Mrs. McMurty will sit in our kitchen while some of the ladies do the dishes and she will finish up the whole of the remainder herself.

Occasionally the ladies will say: "Why don't we take a piece of cake upstairs to Mr. Welch?" and Mrs. McMurty will say: "Don't give him any. I don't approve of husbands working at home. If he were a decent husband he would work downtown." And Dorothy Leighton will say: "If I had a husband who listened at the top of the stairs when I had ladies in, he wouldn't do it more than once, I can tell you!" Green Eyes defends me. She says: "Some men are solitary drunkards, some men run around with other women, worst of all some men play gin-rummy. But my husband just listens at the top of the stairs and I consider it a very minor fault, really."

Last week the PTSA met here, but the PTSA is just about the same group of women who belong to the Garden Club, the Warren-Browning Guild and the Daughters of the Frozen North. Sometimes my downstairs sounds and looks like a supermarket when there's a price war and top sirloin is going for a dollar-nineteen a pound, and I am lucky I have my workroom upstairs and it has a good heavy door to shut.

A couple of ladies came upstairs with a tray for me, coffee and angelfood cake. I have never yet met a man who liked angelfood cake or a woman who didn't, and this may be the main difference between the sexes. So the ladies told me about the handwriting test they were taking downstairs for laughs. They compared one another's handwriting with this chart which Shows Your Character from Your Handwriting. Well it turns out that Mrs. McMurty, who is 40-40-40 straight up and down and looks like a head on Mt. Rushmore, writes slanting very *far* to the right. She turned out to be the sexiest woman in the crowd. This is sure going to surprise her husband when I tell him this evening at the Peabodys' where we are both going to stop by for kerosene highballs on our way to a progressive Republican dinner. I don't mean the Republicans are progressive, I mean the *dinner* is progressive – caviar at one home, turtle soup at the next, filet mignon at a third, crepes at the fourth, etc. A typical Republican-type family dinner. I do not expect to belong to this group because one of Green Eyes' uncles once voted for Truman and that disqualifies us. It's not that we are not nice people, you understand, it just means we are unstable.

Well, anyway, from her handwriting Mrs. McMurty is not only terribly sexy but her tall *t*'s betray the fact that she also has torrid fantasies and day dreams that make up for what is missing in real life with her banker husband.

But the real shocker was The Widow. Her handwriting shows she has no sex appeal at all. She writes downhill which means iron-poor blood, and she writes straight up and down which means she is objective, intellectual and perfectly controlled, and an occasional slant left means she is reserved and cautious.

Now here is a woman who, when she walks around the neighborhood in her tight sweater and pants and is a sister to all the fellows working on their lawns, why work simply stops, that's all. I mean the way The Widow walks is poetry in motion, and now suddenly her handwriting shows it is all empty promise!

I ask the ladies who brought me coffee what Green Eyes' handwriting showed and they wouldn't tell me. Now I'm wondering. I went to the head of the stairs and listened and tried to get a hint, but by then they were talking about a big drive the PTSA was planning to raise money for its overseas missions. The Fullers were in Europe two years ago and they brought back a double basket and harness that work dogs wear in France, and Mrs. Fuller proposed that her dog, Wetter, wear the baskets and accompany the marching PTSA mothers on their rounds from door to door and people would be delighted to put their donation in Wetter's baskets.

I told Green Eyes later: "Mrs. Fuller is out of her flipping head. If people open their front doors to talk to the Marching Mothers and Wetter, there won't be a rug safe in the whole neighborhood." But the PTSA thought it was a terribly *charming* idea and so original, and Wetter started out one evening with Mrs. Fuller and Mrs. Thorndyke. The first place they stopped was the Hixlys', and the minute the door was opened Wetter was in, baskets and all, reconnoitering. Well, not reconnoitering, actually. I am using the word in a rather loose sense.

Mr. Hixly was furious because they have a plain, light-gold rug in their living room and they were not particularly interested in having any design added to it. "I will call up my lawyer and have the PTSA sued tomorrow!" Mr. Hixly shouted, and Mrs. Fuller said: "Oh, for heaven's sake, it's way off in a corner where nobody can see it." And Mrs. Thorndyke said to Mr. Hixly: "I am not accustomed to being addressed by anyone in the tone of voice you are using and I shall certainly tell my husband how you received us." And Mr. Hixly, who was quite out of control, yelled: "If your husband comes around here I'll punch him right in the nose."

What I am saying is that suddenly the PTSA became a disruptive influence in the neighborhood. Well, the ladies left and the next house was the Coopers' and Mrs. Fuller held Wetter quite tightly on his leash. But when Mrs. Cooper opened the front door, Wetter yanked Mrs. Fuller inside and scored on the hall tree and the umbrella jar before Mrs. Fuller quite realized what was happening. Mrs. Cooper burst into tears of indignation because the hall tree was made by her boy when he was innocent and in a shop class at school, before he grew up and started living with a cocktail waitress. The hall tree keeps falling over when you puts hats and coats on it but it has sentimental value for Mrs. Cooper. It reminds her of when her boy loved Mama more than anyone. So they finally had to take Wetter home and get Fifi, The Widow's poodle who is a perfect lady, to carry the baskets, but irreparable damage to the fund drive had already been done.

* * *

It seems to me that the women around here get most of their exercise going around the neighborhood collecting money for drives. Right now The Widow is working for a downtown charity and in the evening she goes from house to house leaving little envelopes to be filled with pennies, and then she comes around again to pick them up.

I do not believe the wives are wholly in sympathy with The Widow's charity. As Mrs. McMurty says, The Widow comes around to collect during the cocktail hour when the husband of the house is home and when the wife is in the kitchen cooking dinner and the husband can be expected to open the door.

Mr. McMurty opened the door the other evening when he was halfway through his usual two-quart pitcher of martinis and there was The Widow, and he cried out heartily: "Why, hello there, Neighbor! You're just in time for a fix."

Now I want to tell you why I think The Widow is a virtuous person. She said: "Is your charming wife at home?" And Mr. McMurty, who can be jolly even if he is a retired banker, said: "Yes, darn it, but she is in the kitchen getting dinner. That's why I'm drinking this. To cut the grease."

Well, Mrs. McMurty knew good and well who was in the front room with Mr. McMurty, but she pretended she didn't and she hollered from the kitchen: "Are you talking to yourself again, you old goat?" And The Widow said: "Well, thanks, it's been lovely, but this is where I came in."

Then Mrs. McMurty threw Mr. McMurty's clothes out the second-story window onto the lawn again – it happens two, three times a week – and he went over to the Dibbles' for dinner. The Widow had stopped by there, too, for an envelope, and Mrs. Dibble was saying to her: "I didn't know that was the kind of uniform you are supposed to wear when you work for your charity. My recollection of the correct uniform is that it makes you look like a woman sergeant in the Canadian Army." The Widow was wearing tight pants and T-shirt, about two sizes tight. And The Widow said: "When I come home I like to change into something more comfortable." And Mrs. Dibble said: "In that outfit, what's the comfort? I have seen wallpaper that is looser."

So The Widow came to our house for our envelope and Green Eyes invited her to dinner. I don't think Green Eyes trusts me completely, but like she said at the Garden Club: "If you've got the kind of husband you could lose to another woman, the sooner it happens the better."

* * *

I want to tell you how one of our most exclusive women's groups got started years ago. They call themselves now the Browning-Warren Guild, and I don't think women who have moved into the neighborhood recently and hope desperately they will be asked to join have any idea it started with bumper strips. Years ago Mr. McMurty incautiously told his wife that he admired Chief Justice Earl Warren, and naturally Mrs. McMurty hated Warren from that moment because it is a rule with her to hate anything her husband is for.

At that time some soreheads were talking about impeaching the chief justice and were putting "Impeach Earl Warren" bumper strips on their cars. So Mrs. McMurty got some bumper strips and talked some of her women friends into putting them on their cars and starting an Impeach Earl Warren Club. They met two or three times, but soon they ran out of things to say about Earl Warren. After all, he seemed like a good family man who didn't run around with fan dancers and imperil the country. So one of the ladies brought an old book of poems by Elizabeth Barrett Browning to a meeting and read them aloud, and the ladies were delighted with poems that were about romantic love and rhymed in iambic pentameters, and they decided they would add an inspirational touch to their meetings by reading one of Mrs. Browning's poems each time.

Pretty soon there was nothing left to do about Warren. The members had all written their senators and congressmen and got letters back saying: "Thank you for your interesting letter and I am always glad to hear from you good people back there in my favorite state." But Earl Warren still looked pretty secure up there on the Supreme Court bench, and mostly the club was reading Elizabeth Barrett Browning at meetings.

Some members wanted to change the club name to The Browning Society but Mrs. McMurty said they must not forget their original reason for organizing, so they decided to call it "The Elizabeth Barrett Browning and Impeach Earl Warren Society." This was a long title for their letterhead so they had "The Elizabeth Barrett Browning" in large letters and underneath, in smaller type, "and Impeach Earl Warren Society."

I guess they would have gone on that way except a new hospital group moved into the neighborhood looking for a local chapter. Well, The Elizabeth Barrett Browning and Impeach Earl Warren Society had by far the choicest membership, and the hospital group enrolled the whole organization as a neighborhood guild. So Mrs. McMurty and the executive committee changed the name – it cost them $78 in new stationery alone – to make it read "The Elizabeth Barrett Browning and Impeach Earl Warren *Guild*," which pleased everyone but the hospital's board of trustees. There was the biggest rhubarb you ever heard. Mrs. McMurty, who keeps a list of subversives, including her own husband, listed everybody on the hospital board and parent guild as communists.

So the name was changed to the Browning-Warren Guild, and now there is nothing greater a woman can ask of life than to be accepted as a member.

Green Eyes never belonged to the Guild because she didn't like the way it started, but we were invited to a Browning-Warren Guild party recently, a masquerade party. Green Eyes went as Typhoid Mary and I went as a Bastard Son of Henry the Eighth. People were formally announced, and I knew that when I was announced as a Bastard Son I would be the Life of the Party. And this happened. There wasn't a man present who didn't come to me immediately and say jovially: "Well, how are you, you old Bastard Son of Henry the Eighth?" And at the bar: "Fix another drink for this old Bastard Son of Henry the Eighth."

The other socially important ladies' club in our neighborhood is the Igloo Chapter of the Daughters of the Frozen North. Green Eyes doesn't belong to this either because she once incautiously said she wondered what Freud would make of a group of women who chose extreme cold – frigidity – to symbolize themselves in an organizational way.

Mrs. Piedmont is the Chief Priestess of the Aurora Borealis of the local chapter and gets to wear a train on her long, white goddess gown. Mrs. Fumbles was recently installed as the First Lady of the Ice Flows, one of the lesser offices, but they wanted to be sure she would continue to provide her marvelous salads for their social affairs. At their meetings the ladies all wear long, white goddess dresses and tiaras and jeweled pins that show their degrees in terms of Fahrenheit temperatures. Those above zero are Janes-come-lately, but those below freezing are long-time members and maybe officers.

* * *

The Garden Club has decided to have longer meetings. The new schedule is to gather at 11:00 A.M., clean up old business, read minutes, then luncheon at 12 o'clock. Resume at 1:30 P.M. for new business and adjournment, maybe, at 3:00 P.M.

This means, if I am to eavesdrop on them, I will have to stand at the top of the stairs pretty near four hours! I just don't have that kind of time.

I can already hear you saying," You don't have to listen while they eat lunch." That's all you know about it. Some of the best things I hear are said while they eat.

For instance, at the last meeting while they were eating dessert (under the old schedule), I heard Mrs. McMurty say that when Mr. McMurty addressed the Chamber of Commerce that week on "The Future of the City," he was wearing a pair of shorts with a hole in them you could put a fist through. Instead of getting shorts out of his drawer as usual, he was in a hurry and grabbed the torn shorts from a chair where she had put them aside for the ragbag.

"I found out too late for him to change," Mrs. McMurty said, "and all during the time I knew he was making this big speech and people were listening to him respectfully, I kept thinking about the hole in his shorts." I doubt Mrs. McMurty would have brought this up if the meeting had been in session, but when she is eating her mind starts to wander. Well, at the next meeting Mrs. McMurty was sitting near Mrs. Overby at lunch and heard her telling how her husband got mad at a bad decision on the TV ballgame the night before and Mrs. Overby said: "He was simply furious. He saw *red!*" And Mrs. McMurty, who keeps a file on subversives, made a note of that, and openly accused Mrs. Overby, when she was passing the rolls, of being married to a communist.

After the ladies got calmed down enough to finish lunch and start the meeting again, Mrs. Overby gave a talk on trees and their problems, the ones that have aphids or plug up sewers, and the Siberian elm that drops messy seeds. Mrs. McMurty interrupted: "Do you have a Siberian elm?" And Mrs. Overby said: "Oh, no, I just mentioned it." And Mrs. McMurty said: "I don't know why you found it necessary to mention it. I shouldn't imagine many people would want them around."

So then Mrs. Overby went on: "Among the more desirable trees is the Russian olive. It has small, fragrant flowers that are yellow and silvery, and the foliage is an attractive gray."

And then Mrs. McMurty's voice boomed in: "I think that is quite enough about the Russians. I am *very* much interested in Mrs. Overby bringing a Russian olive tree and Siberian elm into a discussion before a group of one hundred percent loyal American women – I hope."

Well, they had to adjourn in a hurry, but Mrs. Overby stayed behind and said to Green Eyes: "I wish Mrs. McMurty hadn't interrupted me. The nicest part was coming. I was going to tell about the Painted Lady Butterfly whose larvae eat Canadian thistles but don't touch vegetables, fruit and flowers." And Green Eyes said: "I'm glad you didn't mention Canadian thistles. Mrs. McMurty has Canada on her doubtful list, too."

The trouble with listening to these meetings is that they won't let me come down and add my comments. Like the day Mrs. Cooper read a paper about how to attract fairies to your garden. On this occasion, Mrs. Cooper was reading from a book, *"A Witch's Guide to Gardening,"* by Dorothy Jacob, and it occurred to me – do we really *want* fairies in our gardens around here? What happens to our property values when word gets around town that we are the fairy section of the city? As far as I know, and I am very quick at detecting fairies, we have none at the moment. Oh to be sure, Mr. Fuller has a cast-iron gnome and two cast-iron ducks under the lilac bush in his back yard, and sometimes, on a Sunday afternoon when he has been drinking beer, he will profess to see a fairy, as well, among them and he will talk to her at length, but this doesn't count. The kind of fairy I mean is with the tiara, the white ruffled dress, twinkling shoes and scepter. The fairy Mr. Fuller sees looks more like a bathing beauty, he says.

Mrs. Cooper told the Garden Club, if you want to see fairies in your garden you must drink a potion made of salad oil, rosewater, crushed marigolds, thyme and anything you care to throw in, just as you do in making an exotic salad dressing. She said she had concocted a similar solution recently without the oil, and gave it to her husband in his martini, and he liked it and asked for another, double, and he took her out to dinner and a movie, where he sat with his arm around her for the first time in years but went sound asleep and did not see any fairies. She said she was afraid she had used too much rosewater.

* * *

There is only one club for men in our neighborhood, The Nature Study Club. It is a very informal group, open membership for all the fellows who care to attend meetings. We get together on Sundays in somebody's back yard when we have finished mowing our lawns in summer, or watching the TV ball game in winter, and we study grain in its distilled form. Sometimes we study hops in malted beverages or the uses of the juniper berry as a flavoring, and sometimes the pressing of the grape. Very educational.

The wives have a kind of women's auxiliary. I don't know what they call it, but we fellows call it the Come-Home-Now-Charlie Society because invariably in the midst of a meeting the wives show up, one by one, and say: "It's time to come home now, Charlie." I will say this for the Auxiliary. Almost any time a wife tells some Charlie that it is time he went home, she is right as rain.

CHAPTER 2

The Social Life

Like I keep telling you, this is a peculiar neighborhood. You turn up a rock and there's a citizen. At a party the other night this lady comes up and starts to tell me a cute story about her cat, in the course of which she discloses that her husband always sits down on the floor to dress.

The way she started was this: "It's the cutest thing about our cat. My husband was sitting on the floor putting on his pants and Kitty walks in . . ." And I said: "Wait a minute, hold on there! What is this business about your husband sitting on the floor to put his pants on?" And she said: "Yes, he always does." And I said: "He never stands up when he puts his pants on? He never sits on a bed to put his pants on?" And she said: "No. He sits on the floor when he puts on his shorts and his pants, and, also, his shoes and socks."

And I said: "Have you had him to a doctor?" And she said: "I don't believe it is necessary. We've talked about it. It's just something left over from childhood. When he was learning to dress himself, he sat on the floor and he never saw any reason to change. His folks were very social and seldom home, and he was brought up by maids and nobody bothered to teach him to put on his pants any other way. He never went away to school

McCAUSLAND

or anything, so by the time I got him the pattern was pretty well established."

And I said: "I should think the army would have changed that."

And she said: "He was between wars."

And I said: "How does he undress?" And she said: "He loosens his pants so they fall to the floor, then he sits on the floor and pulls them off after he takes off his shoes. The same thing with his socks and shorts. I have to pick them up."

I never did learn what the cat did. Probably the cat just came in to stare disbelievingly.

At parties you learn about people. At this same party a dignified lady disclosed to Green Eyes that her husband had bought a compass and has aligned his bed on a true magnetic pole axis. It meant that the bed stood out from the wall diagonally, and it raised hob with the room's appearance. But the fellow sleeps more soundly now, the wife said, because the magnetic pole is no longer trying to pull him into its axis. The lady said she experienced no difference, herself, and had concluded that electrically she was negative.

"My husband," she said "will walk across a new carpet and build up so much static electricity that a spark will jump a full foot from his hand to a doorknob. But it never happens to me. I guess I am just blah."

* * *

I got into my corset the other night and went to a Civic Function with Green Eyes. The reason I went is that she has this new dress and hasn't had a chance to wear it since I came down with back trouble.

Since she got this dress she has put it on twice and worn it around the house while I was lying in bed with an icebag on my back, and she has hummed in it and done dance steps and carried on imaginary conversations with handsome men with black, piercing, leering eyes. A fellow would be a fool to let her go to a party alone in that mood.

She wasn't going to go to the party, she was going to stay home with me like a *pal*. Wild horses wouldn't have pulled her away. But she put on the dress that evening and got perfumed up and was walking around the house being vivacious and I said to myself: "I am going to take her to that party if I have to slither on my stomach. I have an investment in that dress, and in her, and a fellow has to protect his investments. And anyway, maybe I should go out and let other people tell me that their backs hurt worse than mine, which is ridiculous."

So I got into this corset thing, which is like sewing up a turkey. I have the greatest sympathy for every woman who ever had to get into a corset or girdle if it is anything like mine. I immediately had to scratch. I was standing there at the Civic Function scratching tentatively, but it did no good and a Big Mouth came along and said: "How's everything out at the monkey house?"

Then this lady came up and said: "You are standing here so stiffly. What's the matter, you don't like this party? You think we're a bunch of slobs or something?" And I said: "I am not even thinking about you, I am thinking about my sore back and this corset I got on."

Then she was crazy to know about the corset and so were some other women who came along. I looked around for Green Eyes, but she is never there when I need her at parties. I said to the lady: "It's just like a girdle, that's all." And she said: "How do you keep it from riding up?" And I said: "There are straps." And she said: "How do straps work?" And I said: "I don't ask about your girdle, why do you ask about mine? I am not going to tell you about the straps." And another lady said: "Can I feel you through your coat?" And I said: "Certainly not!" But she poked me anyway, and they all poked me and said: "He's like a battleship."

Green Eyes all this time was across the room posing in her new dress and finally she came over to me and said: "Well, what do you know, Casanova! I hear all the ladies have been around you like flies."

Then she drove me home and helped me get the corset off – actually there is a button I push and I am ejected like a jet pilot – and she rubbed my back until I went to sleep.

But she was entitled to the evening and the pressure is off her now. The next time it will be just another dress to her and I won't have to get out of a sickbed to show it off.

* * *

I don't think I will ever understand women's ideas about social life. Sometimes I think I almost understand them, and then something happens. Like the other night. I wanted to buy dinner for someone, and I asked Green Eyes to call the lady and ask her if she and her husband were free for the evening.

So Green Eyes phoned this lady and identified herself. And then she said how nice it was to be talking to this lady again. And the lady on her end of the line said yes, wasn't it.

And then Green Eyes said how were the ladies' grandchildren? And the lady said her grandchildren were coming along fine and they were just wonderful. And then Green Eyes gave the lady a run-down on *our* grandchildren. You know, she told the lady about Cute Things.

No mention yet about going out to dinner, and already the conversation had run *eight minutes*.

And I shouted at Green Eyes: "For heaven sake, when are you going to *ask* her? Maybe her dinner is already cooking while you are talking to her!"

And Green Eyes said: "Oh, shut up!" and the lady said: "Hahzat?" And Green Eyes said: "I was talking to my husband who is shouting at me." So then Green Eyes said: "Oh, this weather! Isn't it awful? I just feel so gloomy." And the other lady said yes, she felt gloomy, too. The lady said she had just got a letter from her daughter in Chicago, and, believe it or not, the weather was *worse* there. And Green Eyes said: "It can be terrible sometimes in Chicago."

And I shouted: "Chee-e! *When* are you going to ask her if she and her husband can go to dinner with us tonight?" And Green Eyes said to me: "Look, let me handle this, will you?" And I said: "Chee-e, you never get around to it."

And Green Eyes said to the lady: "I haven't seen you at the Symphony meetings." And the lady told her sometimes the Symphony meetings were a miserable bore, and Green Eyes said, yes, the last speaker was dull, dull, dull. And the lady said some of the meetings can be so dull a person falls right to sleep.

And I said: "Will you, for heaven sake, hang up? Let me call her husband. I can take care of it in fifteen seconds."

And Green Eyes said to the lady: "I am afraid my husband is getting a little impatient. He wants to know if you and Joe would like to go out to dinner with us tonight?" And the lady said: "We would simply love to." And Green Eyes turned to me and said: "They would love to." And she went right back to asking the lady should they wear long skirts or pant suits and the lady gave her a long description of a pant suit she had just bought and would love to wear because it simply took pounds off her. And then it took another five minutes to set the time.

When they got done I asked Green Eyes: "Why didn't you ask her when you first called instead of all that jazz about grandchildren and weather and the Symphony?"

And Green Eyes said: "Don't you talk to me that way. You just don't phone another woman and ask her bluntly to go somewhere. You've got to observe the social niceties." And I said: "Pooh on social niceties!" Well, that's an approximation of what I said. And Green Eyes said: "I know I can never make you understand, but when you've got something to say to another woman, you've got to visit a little first."

I want to tell you how I would have handled the same job with the lady's husband. I would have called him: "Hello, Stupid, are you doon anything tonight?" And he would have said: "No. What you got in mind?" And I would have said: "Dinner. You be at my house at seven for booze, and then we'll go out for dinner. And I'll lie to you and you'll lie to me, and we'll both be Big Men. Bring your wife."

And he would say: "It's the best offer I've had today. Keep a lamp in the window."

No nonsense, no horsing around. The facts on the line. That's the way men talk. But I don't know, when I see Green Eyes all dressed up to go out to dinner, I find myself very glad she is a woman and not a fella, even if she does run all around the ball park when inviting another couple to dinner.

* * *

We had this Slave Auction at the Legion Hall and the fellows got a chance to bid on other fellows' wives to be their slaves for one hour, and the proceeds went to charity. The Equal Rights Amendment went clean out the window, but for a good cause.

I want to tell you, the neighborhood won't be the same for another month or so. I know three wives who went off to live with their mothers because their husbands bid them so low, and I know a couple of husbands who were shocked right down to their shoelaces to find other fellows bidding up to thirty dollars for their wives.

All the wives did, you understand, was serve a basket dinner, al fresco, to their "masters" who bid them in, and speak nice to them, and like that. I don't want you to think our neighborhood would condone any other kind of behavior. We may be corny, but, thank heaven, we are not immoral.

I do believe that Mr. Dibble would be immoral if anyone gave him a chance, but his wife watches him too closely. Also, he telegraphs his moves. If he is making a great play for a strange lady, why he puts her on her guard by pinching her somewhere along the line. Two drinks and Mr. Dibble starts pinching like a conductor's punch on a commuter ticket to the city.

It has been my experience that when you pinch a lady, it abruptly dissolves whatever romantic mood she may be in. Mr. Dibble hasn't learned this yet. Some men never do.

I am not the smartest fellow in the world, but I am smart enough to know that when wives are being auctioned, a fellow had better bid higher than anyone else for his *own* wife or he is in big, fat trouble. All the other husbands went to the auction determined to bid on The Widow, but I knew from the start that I was going to bid in Green Eyes no matter what it cost me, and I also knew that I was going to make my first bid at least a dollar more than the winning bid on The Widow. It is because I am so intuitive about things like this that I eat better than most other husbands in our neighborhood, and never once has Green Eyes thrown my clothes out of an upstairs window onto the front lawn like some other fellows I know.

Mrs. McMurty was first on the auction block, and although she bothers me, I felt sorry for her. The bidding on her was real slow even though she puts up a gourmet lunch. I went over to Mr. McMurty and said: "If you don't bid twenty-five dollars for your wife I am going to kick you in the slats," and he knew I meant it. So he did, and she looked very pleased and ate hardly anything for dinner. I do believe that if Mr. McMurty would only love her a little more she might become thin and almost human.

Mr. Dibble won The Widow. He paid thirty-eight dollars for her. And Mrs. Dibble, who brought only eighteen dollars herself and had to spend an hour with a new neighbor who very seldom speaks, said: "If he pinches you just once, I will kill him." And The Widow said: "I will hold you to that promise."

My first bid for Green Eyes was thirty-nine dollars and she said – right up there on the stage – : "How long you going to be around town, there, sailor?" Thirty-nine dollars sounds extravagant, but she only gives me ten dollars a week to spend, so she had to pay nearly all of the thirty-nine dollars herself because it was Thursday night and I was down to two dollars and thirteen cents. But she didn't seem to mind.

The Widow made Dibble keep both hands on the table where she could see them, and she spoon-fed him, and was a little rough about it, too.

People often ask me, do we have any culture around our neighborhood. Culture? Certainly we have culture. Can you imagine any evening more cultural than this?

* * *

I had to go to Dr. Excerebro's house the other night and look at movies he made of his grandson going the first day to kindergarten, and the next time Green Eyes gets me into an evening like that, I may leave her.

Dr. Excerebro is a terrific brain surgeon. He is mostly noted for the time he was on a hunting trip and it was his turn to stay in camp and get dinner for the gang, and when they came back they found he had taken a few spare hours in the afternoon to remove his own gallbladder. (Had a good dinner ready, too.) Used a hand mirror and a few tools out of the camper. A great talent, really, and, the funny thing, he shakes all over—continuously. We call him "Old Shakey," but they say when he gets a scalpel and a trephine in his hands, with a surgical nurse holding each arm still, there isn't a better neuro-surgeon in the country.

Green Eyes said "yes" when Mrs. Excerebro called to say she was having some of the neighbors in to see pictures of the first grandchild going to kindergarten. Green Eyes said to me: "Now, you have certain obligations when you live in a nice neighborhood like this, and you can't withdraw continually from what you think is cornball. I am sure the doctor will have some good drinks and Mrs. Excerebro will set a nice buffet." And I said: "All the booze in the world will not anaesthetize enough to make one of his clambake movies bearable." And Green Eyes said: "The McMurtys are going and the Dibbles, and if they can stand it, so can you." My own wife, a Judas goat!

I remember once I saw a girl in one of Dr. Excerebro's movies, and she was doing the sexiest bouncing dance I ever saw, and I said to Green Eyes: "Gee, look at that babe at the right end of the line. *Va-room!*" And she said: "She's standing still. She's not dancing. It's the camera that's shaking." And so it was. Old Shakey at his artistic best.

McMurty came over with a pitcher of martinis before we went and a good thing he did – bankers are more foresighted than most people – because Mrs. Excerebro said at the door: "Now we are not going to have drinks before the pictures because these are so cute that I don't want a lot of inattention and drunken guffaws and like that." And Dibble, who hadn't been previously anaesthetized, looked like somebody had thrust a spear right through his chest. He crumpled. He began to wave and his wife said: "What is this all about?" And he said: "I am waving from the tumbril as I am being carried to the guillotine."

As the doctor set up his projector, Mrs. Excerebro said: "The first sequence is of Bobby-Bob – we call him Bobby-Bob – eating his breakfast and throwing his oatmeal at his mother. Then he leaves in his mother's car and sticks his little tongue out at the camera. Then there is a wonderful sequence where he kicks his new kindergarten teacher in the shin, and she kicks him back, so cute, lots of action . . ."

And just then the telephone rang and it was the hospital and an emergency. Oh, brother, sometimes the sun does shine, sometimes the birds do sing and sometimes the governor's pardon arrives in time. We put Old Shakey in his car and watched him bounce from curb to curb onto the freeway, and the films were postponed because Mrs. Excerebro didn't know how to run the projector and not a single one of the rest of us did either!

I feel kind of sorry for Dr. Excerebro these days. He has a son in medical school, his second year, and already the kid is writing home that his father is old-fashioned. The kid knows all the new answers and writes that Dad should study up. It is rough on Old Shakey to get underlined lecture notes on brain surgery from the kid. As a matter of fact, Dr. Excerebro is in the books himself. He has perfected a number of operations, including one on the inner ear which shuts out television commercials. He drills a hole, then plugs it. It's known everywhere as the "closed window" operation and produces a blissful state known medically as "cocktail party ear," where you don't hear anything that is said to you and all you have to do to keep a conversation going is to nod in affirmation from time to time and wear a wide grin. I am saving up for one of these operations myself.

* * *

The telephone rang while I was working at home one day and I answered, and the voice on the other end was heavily weighted with hostility. I recognized the lady at once, it was Mrs. McMurty.

Mrs. McMurty said: "I would like to talk to your wife, please." And I said: "She is shopping down at the village." And Mrs. McMurty said: "Well, it certainly is going to do me no good to talk to *you*." And I said: "Oh, I don't know. Try me." And she said: "I was trying to find out who was having the party." And I said: "I know there is a party because I see all the automobiles parked along the curb on both sides of the street, but I don't know what house the party is in."

And Mrs. McMurty said: "Did you notice which way the ladies walked?" And I said: "No, I didn't." And she said: "You are usually so nosy I thought you'd know *exactly* where they were going."

Her problem was her driveway was blocked and she wanted to get her car out of the garage, so I went over there to see if I could jockey some of the parked cars out of the line. I couldn't. Every lady had her car locked on Mrs. McMurty's side of the street, and Mrs. McMurty was terribly anxious to get to a meeting of a group she belongs to which is preparing for the day when the Republicans rise and come marching down our street.

So I said to Mrs. McMurty (didn't expect her to do it): "It looks to me as if the only way you can get your car into the street is to drive up the sidewalk to the end of the block." And that is exactly what she did. But she didn't quite make it all the way. Dorothy Leighton had left the end of her car projecting out of her driveway over the sidewalk, and Mrs. McMurty clipped it pretty good. Dorothy Leighton came screaming out of her house just as a police car came by, and Mrs. McMurty was cited for driving on the sidewalk, and Dorothy Leighton was cited for letting her car overhang the sidewalk, and all the ladies at the party who had blocked driveways got tickets, too. *Everybody* was sore and I had a wonderful afternoon.

Mrs. McMurty brooded about this more than somewhat. She went to court and took her lumps and then she visited the city attorney's office to ask whether a homeowner had any priority on the curbside parking space in front of his own home, and the city attorney said no, but it was illegal to block a driveway. Mrs. McMurty said coldly: "Well, it is clear enough to me that I am talking to a Democrat," and she stamped out of the office.

She then went to a sign shop and had several signs made. One said: "Reserved for McMurty" and the other said "Violation to Park Here." She put them on her driveway and parking strip that evening. When Blair came home he parked in front of the McMurtys' because he has three cars and a two-car garage, but he was careful not to block the driveway. He pulled up the "Reserved for McMurty" sign and moved it ten feet further along the McMurty lot, and Mrs. McMurty ran out of the house and put it back while Blair walked into his house and paid no attention. So Mrs. McMurty called the police and they told her to take down the signs. But they told her she could post her sign near her driveway saying "Violation to Block Driveway."

She has about six signs over there this very minute, and Mr. McMurty is over at the Blairs having a drink and being jolly, and Mrs. McMurty just called Green Eyes to say she is having a mass meeting at her house to discuss the parking crisis, and Dorothy Leighton is having one, too, to protest Mrs. McMurty getting everybody else pinched. There is nothing like a party to divide a neighborhood.

CHAPTER III

Some People Who Help

I always attend Mr. Hapsburg, the TV serviceman, when he fools around with our set because if you don't watch him, he makes all the girls' legs look fat. He's from the Old World, down the Balkans somewhere, and his idea of feminine beauty runs to fat legs. The last time he was at our house he made the New York City Ballet dancers look like they were walking around on pickle kegs.

"It is just a bad tube," he said this time, and I said: "Okay, and don't fool around with the settings because I don't want the girls to have fat legs. Every time you are here I have to get some other serviceman to come in and change the girls' legs back to the way I like them."

And he said: "You want the girls' legs to look like they are starving to death? A healthy girl should have strong, healthy legs." And I said: "I do not want to see a bunch of peasants beetling around when I turn on my television. I do not care for girls who look like they should have a broom and be sweeping the street outside the Moscow railroad station."

Well, it did me no good. That night Mary Tyler Moore was three feet wide and three feet high and I had to get in the back of the set and risk electrocution to adjust her to normal. She thanked me for it, too.

But while he was here, Mr. Hapsburg asked me what shows I look at because he was making his own survey.

"Do you look at 'Emergency'?" he asked me, and I said: "No. Mostly I look at the educational channel." And he said:

McCAUSLAND

"Everybody says they look mostly at the educational channel, but they don't." And I said: "But *I do*." And he said: "If you look mostly at the educational channel, why do you worry about how the girls legs look?"

And I said: "Because they have ballet on the educational channel often and I like to watch the girls dance." And he said: "the legs shouldn't make any difference." And I said: "You look at ballet your way and I will look my way."

And he said: "What other programs do you like on Educational TV?" And I said: "I like any ones about cooking: French, Italian, Chinese." And he said: "They're no good. Hungarian cooking is the only cooking that's any good." And I said: "You are not supposed to get your own ideas into a survey. What good is a survey if it's your ideas?"

The truth is, Mr. Hapsburg doesn't like anything on TV except symphony and there isn't any American symphony orchestra he likes, either. He will come to fix your TV set and before he starts he will ask: "Are you sure you want this fixed?" Mr. Hapsburg is almost as disenchanted with people as Mr. Pritchard, the morose plumber who is sad because women call a toilet a "john," which is his given name. Mr. Hapsburg is disenchanted with manufacturers, too. He told me there was a set on the market a while back on which the tuning slugs were light plastic and broke after very little use, and he had to fix them with chewing gum. And I said: "You're kidding." And he said: "No. There are tuning slugs threaded through plastic disks, and when they break you put them back and hold them in position with chewing gum and modeling clay, then fill with plastic mix. And this is what is wrong with America. You pay five hundred dollars for a color set and you have to repair it with chewing gum."

* * *

Mr. Pritchard is having a little wife trouble. Mrs. Pritchard read in a plumbers' magazine that plumbers should think of themselves as doctors – responding to emergency calls, available to care for any illness of a plumbing system – and now she insists he must call himself Doctor and respond to calls just as a physician does.

The other night the Fullers had an emergency and called the plumber. Mrs. Pritchard answered the phone and Fuller said: "Could Mr. Pritchard come over right away? My whole basement is flooded." Mrs. Pritchard said: "Dr. Pritchard takes night calls only in extreme emergency. Perhaps some younger plumber would do. Are you one of Dr. Pritchard's regular clients?" And Mr. Fuller said: "We sure are and this is a real emergency. We are about to float away." And Mrs. Pritchard said: "Very well, I'll awaken Plumber."

When Pritchard came to the phone he had Fuller describe the trouble, then he said: "I see. What is the temperature of the water?" And Fuller said: "It's lukewarm." And Pritchard said: "Did this start with a dampness around the water heater?" And Fuller said: "Yes, we began to notice dampness yesterday morning." And Pritchard said: "I shouldn't worry about it too much. There have been a number of cases of flooded basements around town recently."

And Fuller shouted: "But the water is already up to my ankles." And Pritchard said: "What color is it?" And Fuller said: "It's the color of any water in a dirty basement." And Pritchard said: "I suggest you shut off the water at the main valve and turn off the gas or electricity to the tank and take two aspirins and go to bed. I'll talk to my receptionist at the shop in the morning and see if I can fit you into the afternoon."

By that time Fuller was screaming: "You mean you're not coming right away?" And Pritchard said: "Call me tomorrow and tell me how you are doing. You may have a little dampness that will persist for a few weeks. If the water continues to rise, however, we will have to consult an associate who specializes in pumping out basements. But let's not cross that bridge until we have to."

Mr. Fuller was so sore he called another plumber and he's been telling everybody since that Mr. Pritchard doesn't know a pipe wrench from a plumbers' snake. So Mr. Pritchard dropped the professional approach and now he won't let his wife answer the phone at night or call him "Doctor."

Mr. Pritchard doesn't want to antagonize his customers because so many men are putting in their own second bathrooms in homes that were built before the multiple-baths period. A friend of mine bought a prewar tri-level with only a bath and a half. He says adding another bath was no trouble at all and increased immensely the value and comfort of his home. Of course, when he turns on the hot water it comes out cold, and when he turns on the cold, it runs hot. But he says you get used to that – just takes some adjustment in habits.

Green Eyes tells me that at a recent Garden Club meeting one of the visiting lady guests said: "Heavens knows, my husband is no mechanic, but he put in a second bathroom in our home last weekend and it seems to work fine. Of course, the pipes all run down outside the house, but we'll conceal them with a clinging vine of some sort."

Every time Mr. Pritchard sees a truck in front of a house around here with a new set of bath fixtures in it, he knows sooner or later he'll be called in to make some sense out of the valves and connections and get the family back to bathing regularly.

Last year Mr. Pritchard was called in by Mr. Phillips to modernize his bathroom and add a second one and, let me tell you, that is one of the most terrible things that can happen to anyone. It means you have no usable bathroom for weeks.

The Phillipses' house was one of the first built in our suburban neighborhood. Actually they moved in, I think, before the Indians were entirely subdued. It's a little house and it still looks good because the architecture is classic, but the kitchen and the one bathroom were years behind the world. Mr. Phillips got tired of the tub with the ball feet and the ceiling flush tank with the long pull chain. Mrs. Fumbles tried to dissuade them from giving up those antiques, insisting they were authentic period pieces, but the Phillipses insisted they had lived long enough with antiques and wanted a few years of enjoying modern plumbing and silent toilets.

If you have only one bathroom and are having it modernized and another added, there are several things you can do. You can first have minimum fixtures installed somewhere, which the Phillipses couldn't do because the new fixtures were not readily available. Or you can have a portable, temporary building erected in the back yard and lower everybody's property values. Or, if the right kind of people live near you, you can run over to the neighbors.

So Mrs. Phillips told Mrs. Blair – up the street two houses – that she just didn't know what they would do while they were having new bathrooms installed. And right away Mrs. Blair said: "Why don't you feel free to use our downstairs bathroom? We have three complete baths." And Mrs. Phillips said: "Oh, I think that is the most kindly, neighborly gesture I ever heard of."

Mrs. Blair thought the Phillipses would be needing her bathroom only a few days. It never occurred to either lady that the fixtures for the Phillipses' house would have to be specially ordered because they were an odd size, and that an outside wall would have to be moved for the new bath. Mr. Pritchard discovered that after the old fixtures were removed.

Mr. Blair considered his downstairs bathroom as his own private retreat, and when Mrs. Blair told him that the Phillipses would be using it for a few days, Mr. Blair was displeased and said: "Fine, that's great, that is! Why do they have to bring their business to *us*?" And Mrs. Blair said: "Shame on you. I want you to be a good sport about it."

Well, the Phillipses would come over from time to time during the day, but on the second day the doorbell rang at midnight and it was Mr. Phillips. So Blair gave Mr. Phillips a key and Mrs. Phillips had a duplicate made and they were coming and going all day and late into the evening. And they would shout: "Yoo, hoo! It's all right. I just came to use the bathroom again." Altogether it went on for three weeks, and it really wasn't much bother except that one night, when the Blairs had the new minister and his wife to dinner, Mrs. Phillips came in and shouted where she was going, and the minister seemed startled.

Then there was the night the Blairs were entertaining the Descendants of the Mayflower and everybody was dressed up to the eyeballs, and Mrs. Phillips came over in jeans and an old sweater to use the powder room. It was in use temporarily, and Mrs. Phillips waited in the hall, and a Mayflower type brought her a drink and a tray of hors d'oeuvres, and she said "thank you" very properly. And the Mayflower type said: "Are you a Mayflower descendant?" And Mrs. Phillips said: "Oh, no, I just came over to use the powder room." When the fellow looked puzzled she added: "We don't have one." And the fellow said: "I would think that would be a frightful inconvenience." And Mrs. Phillips said: "Oh, no, not really. The Blairs are so sweet. They've given us a key."

And this Mayflower type went back to the living room and said to another Mayflower type: "You know, you come into a neighborhood like this and you assume everyone is reasonably well off, and then you suddenly discover some homes don't even have the most primitive sanitary requirements . . ."

The fourth week, though, the Phillipses used a camper parked in the alley behind their home. Mr. Blair towed it home and said one of the fellows in the office was kind enough to lend it for the occasion.

But the funny thing is that when Mrs. Blair went through the checks next month, she found this check which Mr. Blair had written to some camper-rental company, and he couldn't seem to remember writing it. He said give him the check and he would talk to the camper people about it, and he never referred to the matter again. Mrs. Blair says this is typical of him. He just writes out checks with never a thought of what they are for.

When the Phillipses' bathroom was finally completed, the

whole neighborhood trooped in to see it. It has a sunken, tile tub you walk down three steps to get into, and it has a shower and double sink and nine miles of mirror and counter, and a separate facility, and sun lamps and I don't know what. I sure envied the Phillipses this great, big sunken tub. It would be a wonderful place to sail my big, red ferryboat, and the water level could come up even with one of the steps to make a fine wharf. Of course, you would have to sit with your back to the faucets and you could gore yourself on the soap dish. But imagine being able to sit in a bath with water right up around your neck!

Well, the Phillipses were at the McMurtys' one Saturday night, and somebody mentioned their gorgeous new bathroom, and Mrs. Phillips began talking about it in a highly unladylike way. She used vulgar, ugly words that should never pass a lady's lips. The gist of it was that her head must have been screwed on wrong when she let Mr. Pritchard talk her into having a sunken tub. The only way she could clean it was to take off her clothes and get right into the tub. She said the first time her husband walked in while she was cleaning the tub, crawling around on her hands and knees, nude, her husband said: "Whatever *are* you doing?" And she said: "Shut up!" And he said: "Why don't you use a mop with a long handle?" And she said: "You can't scrub off algae between the tiles with a mop, and one more suggestion and I'll let you clean this thing yourself."

Somehow it made all of us feel better with our own modest bathrooms. But I do wish there were a step or shelf in my tub to use as a slip for my ferryboat. It is kind of silly to pretend that your knee is where it docks."

One of these days I'm going to have to put in another bathroom myself, and then Mr. Pritchard will be at my house repairing *my* mistakes. We really don't need another now that our children are married and no longer spending most of their time in our bathroom. I got to wondering what my house is really worth so I asked a real estate fellow to come over and take a look. We built our house years ago and it has architectural and artistic integrity. And I said to the fellow: "What do you think this place is worth?" And he said: "How many baths do you have?"

And I said: "This house is a replica of one built in 1650 and still standing in Deerfield, Massachusetts. Of course, we added a few modern touches." And he said: "How many baths?"

And I said: "For instance, here is an escape hatch near the fireplace through which we can flee if we are attacked by hostiles. And upstairs we have gunports through which we can pour boiling water or hot fat on raiders." And he said: "I suppose you have two full baths, at least."

And I said: "Notice the plank floors with real pegs and the beamed ceilings and the Holy Lord hinges to keep evil spirits away." And he said: "All the buyer wants to know these days is how many baths."

And I said; "As you can see, this is about as Early American as you can get. We live in constant fear that the British will be marching around the bend any day." And he said: "It would help if you told me how many baths."

And I said: "Don't forget, we built this twenty-five years ago and it has the equivalent of two full baths." And he said: "What is the equivalent?"

And I said: "There's a full bath on the second floor, a powder room on the first, and a facility and shower in the basement." And he said: "That's what I was afraid of. You're dead there, Clyde; no master bath, no sauna with your master bedroom."

And I said: "We got along fine. The kids used the basement shower." And he said: "Kids won't do that anymore. If a kid doesn't have his own private bath, the other kids won't talk to him."

"Good heavens, what is that?" he asked when we went through the kitchen." And I said: "It's a double-oven electric stove." And he said: "You mean you got no microwave, no built-in, eye-level ovens, no barbecue?"

So, I guess if I don't get Mr. Pritchard in to figure out some way to save this place – I'll have to burn it down before it is condemned.

* * *

Mr. Sprunt is our bus driver. I don't mean to give the impression that we have only one bus and one bus driver to service our neighborhood, but Mr. Sprunt works a split shift – he's on the 8:20 in the morning and the 5:29 going home. He moonlights in his off hours doing marriage counseling.

Mr. Sprunt is an engaging fellow. He always says: "Hello, there, beautiful," to all the ladies, even the worst hags, and he does recognize when a lady has a new haircut and always volunteers that it is most flattering. This endears him to women who could get their heads shaved and their husbands would never notice.

Mr. Sprunt, poor fellow, has hay fever and he has tried everything for it – ipecac, horseradish (both raw and powdered), quinine, chloroform, rabies shots and, worst of all, garlic pills. I will never forget the garlic pills. Passengers got off the bus about halfway downtown and walked the rest of the way. In the back of the bus we delegated Mr. McMurty to approach Mr. Sprunt delicately and tell him that he "offended."

Mr. McMurty went up to the front of the bus and said: "Sprunt, have you ever seen that television commercial where they put raw onion in a machine and the machine goes whoom, whoom, and the dial goes like crazy?" And Sprunt said: "Yeah, many times." And McMurty said: "Well, Sprunt, when you eat garlic pills you got it beat."

Next morning we let the 8:20 go by and waited for the 8:45, and Sprunt's feelings were hurt terribly. So he gave up the garlic pills and now he is practicing a system of "manipulation" where you are supposed to cure hay fever by pressing your upper lip under your nose very hard when you feel a sneeze coming on or your eyes begin to water. Sprunt drives with his right hand and holds his lip with his left, and when he has to make a turn signal he doesn't have an extra hand to do it so the passengers on the turn side of the bus all put out their arms, and it startles motorists behind to see twenty arms go out the window all at once.

It startled the route supervisor pretty good, too, and he flagged down the outgoing 5:29 last Friday and he asked Mr. Sprunt what was this about driving with one hand. Sprunt began to explain how you can manipulate hay fever away if you press hard and have Good Thoughts, and the supervisor said: "How do you get around that curve on Aaron Burr Drive?" and Mr. Sprunt said: "Generally some lady behind me reaches over my shoulder and pulls the wheel."

The supervisor was going to take him off the bus right there, but McMurty got up and froze the supervisor with a single glance and said coldly: "Are you drunk on duty?" And Blair got up and said: "He looks drunk to me, too. What's your name there, fella?" And the supervisor just vanished, quick.

Now we have a deal where Sprunt uses both hands on the Aaron Burr curve, and the passenger behind him gets up and presses a finger against Sprunt's upper lip while he negotiates.

Mr. Sprunt has a real social consciousness; he feels he must get us safely to and from our homes. Sometimes he waits a good five minutes at the downtown stop for late arrivals and then, because we are at the end of his route, he sometimes drives his bus off his regular street and goes down side streets to let us off at our doorsteps.

I recall Christmas Office Party Night last year. Mr. McMurty sat in the back of the bus without much sign of life when we rolled up to our stop, and Mr. Sprunt went back and shook him and said: "Mr. McMurty, this is where you leave us." And Mr. McMurty said: "I believe I will go back downtown with you. I left my umbrella at the club." And Mr. Sprunt asked me if I would drop McMurty off at his home. And I said: "I will take him to my house, but I am not going to take him to Mrs. McMurty in that condition. She will blame me for it."

So Sprunt turned the bus around and came down my street and let us out. But Mrs. McMurty was waiting on her porch, and for once she wasn't a monster. "The poor man," she said, "he's been at a bank meeting, you know, and he always comes home from those meetings simply exhausted."

* * *

Pretty near everybody in the immediate block in my neighborhood has Mrs. Norberg come in to help with the cleaning once a week or twice a month, or just occasionally when she has an extra day. Green Eyes doesn't. We have Green Eyes' Aunt Bitty when we need an extra hand, and she is seven feet tall and wears men's boots. She also steals and she doesn't clean very good, either, but it's all in the family. She is very strong. During the war she worked in the shipyards and held up ships.

I sometimes ask Green Eyes why she doesn't let Aunt Bitty stay on her chicken farm and hire Mrs. Norberg, instead, but Green Eyes says she will never let Mrs. Norberg organize her the way Mrs. Norberg organizes all the women she works for.

Mrs. Norberg insists that the woman of the house be fully dressed and have breakfast out of the way before she arrives at 8:30. That's okay for the women who go off to work, but for the wives who just lazy around the house all day, Mrs. Norberg, when she comes, lays out the day's work. She tells the lady of the house what she must do while Mrs. Norberg is doing things *she* wants to do, and, if the lady of the house falls behind, Mrs. Norberg can be quite severe.

Green Eyes was having coffee at the Fullers' the other morning and Mrs. Fuller was still in nighty and robe when Mrs. Norberg came. Mrs. Norberg said to Mrs. Fuller: "My, we are late today, aren't we? Let's get to work. You do the kitchen floor today while I do the windows, and then we'll both get at the basement. I told Mr. Fuller last week that I wanted his workbench cleaned up before I came today, and I expect to see he did it." Green Eyes hadn't realized how much of a cooperative effort Mrs. Norberg considered her cleaning job.

Mrs. Norberg cooks the lunch, too. She doesn't trust her employers to cook her the good, healthy, hearty lunch she requires. What the women around here dread most is the carbohydrates they have to eat on Mrs. Norberg's "day." They have to eat what Mrs. Norberg cooks or her feelings will be hurt and she'll cut you off her list. She always brings pie from home, big pies with great crust but thick as your thumb, top and bottom. You never invite a lady in our block to dinner on the day Mrs. Norberg works for her. If you do, she will just sit at the table with her eyes glazed and not touch a thing.

I sat beside Mrs. Blair one night and I thought she looked dejected as she pushed Green Eyes' duck with brandied cherry sauce around on her plate, and she said: "Mrs. Norberg came today and I vacuumed all the rugs and I turned the mattresses and cleaned the kitchen shelves, and for lunch I had to eat this huge, dreadful fish in a thick white sauce, with potatoes and raisin pie, and I am dead." And I said: "What did she do while you were working?" And she said: "I don't know but I think she scrubbed woodwork – right down to the bare wood in some places."

I asked Mrs. Blair why she didn't go out on the days Mrs. Norberg comes, but the ladies who have jobs and aren't home when she comes say that when Mrs. Norberg works alone she is apt to go through all the bureau drawers and put things away where they can't be found and straighten up their accounts and bank books and income tax records, but that is the price they pay for having a clean house.

Once I picked Mrs. Norberg up at the bus stop and drove her right to her own home and I tell you, it *shines*. She told me the women in our neighborhood are pretty much spoiled and she kind of thinks of herself as doing missionary work among them, and I believe she does.

I believe that a woman anywhere in the world would be

overjoyed if her husband brought home a cleaning woman. I believe a fellow could safely bring home a gorgeous cleaning woman in a bikini and nothing would happen except glad cries – provided the cleaning woman in the bikini immediately got out the vacuum cleaner and started to work on the living room shag. I know one instance where a wife in our neighborhood entered her living room and found her cleaning woman – a rather pretty one – combing this wife's husband's hair while he sat with a silly, pleased look on his face, and all the wife said was: "Hilda, the kitchen looks simply sparkling."

Mrs. Fuller has a cleaning woman, and the weird thing is that this cleaning woman has a cleaning woman of her own. I mean while the Fuller's cleaning woman is cleaning the Fuller home there is another cleaning woman cleaning the cleaning woman's home. And sometimes when the Fullers' cleaning woman can't come, she sends *her* cleaning woman as her substitute, but it is understood that the cleaning woman's cleaning woman is to be paid less than the cleaning woman gets.

I sometimes lie in bed at night trying to work out the economics of this. I ask Green Eyes: "If the cleaning woman has to hire a cleaning woman of her own, why doesn't she stay home and do her own cleaning?" And Green Eyes answers: "It makes perfectly good sense to me, but it is not given to a man to understand."

* * *

As I look out the window, I see Mrs. Peterson, a few houses up the street, out on her porch thumbing her nose at Fred, the mailman. Poor Fred. He has passed her again without leaving any mail because there wasn't any for her, and she believes that Fred and his fellow letter carriers at the village substation are engaged in some conspiracy against her.

The truth is she is lonely and lives for her mail. Even when she receives nothing but "occupant" or junk mail, she will read it through to the last word and then sit down and write long, chatty, personal letters to the companies involved. She explains why she can't avail herself of their marvelous, once-in-a-lifetime opportunities, but, she says, she appreciated hearing from them.

When a day or two goes by without Fred leaving some kind of mail she goes to the substation and berates the superintendent. I think it bothers Fred when Mrs. Peterson thumbs her nose at him. He is a kindly man and he wants to be loved by everyone, just as all the rest of us do. He wilts visibly when Mrs. Peterson resorts to this gesture, but I try to console him. I tell him she means nothing personal about it. To her Fred symbolizes not only the federal administration, but also the President, whom, she is certain, always listens in on her phone calls to her sister, Agnes, in South Dakota. When Mrs. Peterson makes her weekly long-distance call to Agnes, she will break right into Agnes' conversation to shout: "Get off the line, there, Mr. President! This is none of your business, snoopy!"

If Captain Peterson would only write more often to his wife when he is away on a voyage, she might be more kind and thoughtful of Fred's feelings. But the only communication she has from her husband is an infrequent gaudy postcard picturing bilious green palm trees on a South Seas island with native girls draped under them and with an inscription: "Having fine time." Not even a "wish you were here." So Fred gets blamed and feels as rejected as Mrs. Peterson does. People just don't realize the complicated human drama that postal service people are faced with in their routine jobs.

CHAPTER IV

Food and Booze

I am never quite sure what kind of wine to serve with red meat and fish and poultry, whether I should serve muscatel or California port. I am not talking about the cheap stuff. I mean a good, vintage muscatel or port from a fine winery, sells for about a dollar thirty-five a bottle. I don't mean a quart, I mean a gallon. If you are going to have people in to a gourmet dinner, I think it is unwise to skimp on the wine, don't you?

Another thing, if you are serving muscatel with filet of sole Amandine and you are pouring from the gallon jug, does one set the gallon jug on the table or is it advisable to keep it on the serving table? I was at a very high class dinner party the other night and the host brought on a gallon jug of fine California port, but in handing it across the table so that his guests could replenish their tumblers, he knocked over two candlesticks and disarranged the beautiful floral arrangement and spilled some wine on the tablecloth and down the pantleg of the guest of honor. The guest, I must say, handled the incident like a man of the world. He looked down at the spreading red stain and said: "I believe I am bleeding to death, but don't bother to call an ambulance until I topple over." I mean, I think a vintage California port tends to bring out the best wit at dinner parties, don't you?

If you are handing a gallon jug across a table to a guest, do you hold it by the handle and let the guest grab it and support it with his two outstretched hands, or do you ask his lady partner to help him? I have never seen this problem discussed in etiquette books.

This port went very well, I think, with the corned beef and cabbage the hostess provided, but, of course, port goes with *anything*. The hostess said her children use it on their pancakes in the morning. Actually, the hostess didn't have much warning that we were all coming to dinner at her house. It was a Sunday evening and her husband had just finished raking leaves in his yard, and he heard some of us fellows, who were doing the same, talking about the day being Mr. Fumbles' birthday. So our host said: "Why don't you bring your wives to my house tonight for a birthday dinner?" And then he went in and told his wife we would be there in an hour, as soon as we had showered, and I understand she created quite a scene in front of the children and I can't understand why.

I think for a while there she was going to pack up herself and the children and go home to mother. There is no understanding women sometimes. They want to plan things for weeks ahead. You find very little spontaneity among them when it comes to having people in to dinner.

"What are you going to give them to drink?" she asked when she calmed down. "There isn't any booze in the house!" And he said: "Have you forgot that gallon of port your father was drinking under the back porch until we took it away from him? We'll have a gourmet dinner with wine." And she said: "It will have to be gourmet corned beef and cabbage, then, because that's what we were having for dinner tonight in the first place." And he said: "The wine will make the difference." And it did.

It's a fact that we are pretty conscious of good manners and proper etiquette in our neighborhood. Mrs. Dibble, for instance, read in a magazine that the really high-class hostess never handles her flatware when setting her table except with white gloves. I don't know whether this would apply only to sterling or to stainless steel and dime store tableware, as well.

I suppose it does. The idea is that there shouldn't be a thumbprint anywhere when a lady guest picks up her fork and turns it over trying to figure how much it cost.

The magazine said that white gloves should be worn even for setting the table for a family meal because white gloves are so elegant and symbolic of good family background, and if you don't have good family background, the white gloves still give an image of it, which is next best.

In the Dibble home, Mrs. Dibble's mother sets the table every night. She is eighty-five and a hearty type – used to own and boss a carnival. She drinks brandy and smokes cigars in bed, and although Mrs. Dibble stoutly denies it, lots of the women around here in the neighborhood have seen the old girl come down for breakfast with cigar ashes on her nighty.

I was at the Dibble home one night watching the old girl set the table, and she carried a couple of spoons over her ears, like a file clerk carries ballpoints. It's a neat trick but easy for her because she has ears like a spaniel. I said to Dibble: "Gee, does the old lady often balance spoons on her ears?" And he said: "Look, Welch, we are having a nice, quiet drink here, so why do you have to louse it up by reminding me of my mother-in-law?"

I guess the old lady is quite a trial. Her favorite adjective for Mr. Dibble is "stupid," and she seldom ever talks to him directly. She talks to him through her daughter. She says: "Tell that stupid husband of yours that he is dribbling applesauce all over his necktie." And Mrs. Dibble says: "Mother, I will not have you constantly calling my husband 'stupid,'" but she doesn't dare protest too much because the old lady owns the house and most everything in it.

Well, Mrs. Dibble brought the white gloves home and told her mother that she thought it would be nice and fashionable if the old lady wore the gloves when she was putting the silverware around the table for dinner. And the old lady said: "Why?" And Mrs. Dibble said: "Because then you don't leave fingerprints." And her mother said: "What's wrong with fingerprints?" And Mrs. Dibble said: "Oh, Mother, you leave fingerprints all over the house, more than the children. It takes me half the week going around getting fingerprints off." And the old lady gave her the clincher: "Who owns this house?"

Mrs. Dibble's mother refused to have any part of the white gloves, so Mr. Dibble wore them the first time. He sat at the head of the table with them on and said: "Now if everybody will hand his silverware to me, we'll get Grandma's fingerprints off it and then we can proceed with this very delectable dinner." And the old lady said to her daughter: "That stupid husband of yours thinks he's a dude."

And Mr. Dibble said: "Your trouble is that you spent so many years with your carnival eating hot dogs and wiping the mustard and grease off the front of your dress that now you are having trouble adjusting to genteel living." And the old lady stood up and hollered, "Hey rube!" – the old carnival rallying cry.

Mrs. Dibble is about to give up the thought of bringing elegance and formality to her dinner table, but I tell you this so you will know the neighborhood has high aspirations.

* * *

My friend Hixly, across the street, used to be a traveling man, and, like his wife says, once a traveling man always a traveling man. She refers to the way he treats sandwiches. He learned long ago, on the road, to lift the top slice of a sandwich and examine the filling carefully. Then to replace the top slice and turn the sandwich over and lift the bottom slice to examine the filling from that side, too. The fellow who is a novice on the road may lift the top slice to look, but it is the old hand who looks at the bottom as well.

Hixly continues to do this with sandwiches – in first-class restaurants, at friends' homes and, even worse, in his own home. "What do you expect to find?" Mrs. Hixly sometimes asks in a fury, and Hixly says: "You never know."

Mrs. Hixly tried to break him of this distressing habit by

giving him open-faced sandwiches, but then he lifts up the filling from the bread with a knife and peers under like a hunter stalking big game. "Can't you even trust your own wife?" she shrieks and he says: "Oh, I don't know."

Hixly won't eat a peanut butter or soft cheese sandwich because you can't peel away the bread and there is no telling what may be in it. "In the old days, in some of the places I had to eat, I have seen a sandwich crawl the whole length of the counter while I was drinking my coffee," he says.

It is funny that odd eating habits can almost bust up a marriage. The Clayborns in the next block from me are an example. They fight mostly about the fact that he likes chocolate pudding better than anything in the world, and Mrs. Clayborn makes it beautifully for him from scratch, rich and dark with chocolate and never a lump in it – and he won't eat it until he beats it into a froth.

This goes back to Mr. Clayborn's childhood, undoubtedly. I have heard him say that his mother never made chocolate pudding without lumps and her mashed potatoes and gravy weren't any better, and the kid grew to manhood expecting to find lumps in anything edible.

Mr. Clayborn will say to his wife: "Why don't we have chocolate pudding any more. You know it's my favorite." And she will say: "You know why. Because you beat up your pudding until no one can sit at the table and look at it. You become an animal." And he says: "I promise I won't beat the next pudding."

So the next night she puts a bowl of chocolate pudding in front of him and says: "I put this through the blender and I beat it half an hour with the whisk and it does *not* have lumps in it." And he changes right there in front of his family, like Dr. Jeykll into Mr. Hyde. He begins to tremble and perspire and he rushes into the kitchen with the bowl and shuts the door and they can hear him whipping his pudding and uttering great cries of gratification. And Mrs. Clayborn breaks out in a psychosomatic rash.

On the other hand, Mrs. McMurty handles rage and food in a different manner. Sometimes when she gets mad at her husband, she throws his clothes out of the upstairs bedroom window onto the lawn. And when she cools down she is contrite and feels that nobody loves her, so she will bake a three-layer chocolate cake and eat the whole thing herself at one sitting – at two o'clock in the morning, maybe.

Dr. Spook, our neighborhood psychiatrist explained this odd behavior to me this way: "Frankly," he said, "it is probably too scientific for you to grasp, but we psychiatrists say that a person who is anxious or hostile or frustrated or a lot of other things has a bird on his head. Sometimes the bird flies away for a while then comes back, sometimes a different bird takes over. But there is always a bird. Mr. Clayborn's is stirring pudding, Mrs. Clayborn's is breaking out in rashes and Mrs. McMurty's is wolfing down chocolate cakes. At the moment I have an eagle on my own head because I am patriotic and high-flying, but I distinctly see a vulture on *your* head because you are always pecking around people's peculiarities and hang-ups."

I think he was wrong. Most of the time my bird is a dove of peace.

* * *

Every woman in our neighborhood thinks she gets better meat from Frank and Joe, our butchers, than they give to *other* women, and how they manage to give women this impression I do not know. I have watched them very carefully at their work and I do believe they are fair and impartial to their lady customers, but I also know that they give The Widow a little edge on the rest. It must be because of the way she leans over the counter at them and wiggles and is a *pal* to them.

I have seen Frank trim two dollars worth of fat off a top sirloin for The Widow and I have seen Joe bone a leg of lamb and tie it up like it was for the king's table. And when The

Widow walks in, Frank or Joe will say: "I have been saving something special for you in the reefer," and she will say: "Oh, you're nice to me," and "you shouldn't have," and like that.

I believe it is because The Widow brightens up their day. The other women come in looking like monsters, wearing pants and car coats with their hair straggling, but The Widow always looks as if she had just stepped off the runway at a fashion show.

I don't believe that The Widow gets great service only because she has a terrific bilt, other women have terrific bilts, too, but The Widow tells Frank and Joe what wonderful butchers they are and the other women with terrific bilts stand

there mentally preoccupied with the rest of the shopping list and their kids pulling things off the shelves, and complain about the cost of hamburger.

The Widow also gets extra service at the big supermarket where the butcher works behind a partition and everything is pre-packaged. I saw her going down the meat counter the other day and I guess the butcher saw her through the window because he was out in a hurry and bowing like a diplomat, saying: "Is there some special cut you'd like because it would be no trouble at all for me to get it for you."

The last time I was in the Blue Ribbon Grocery in the village, The Widow was at the meat counter and Frank, the butcher, was waiting on her and leaning away over the case like he hoped she would fondle his ear. I started to tell Joe, the other butcher, what Green Eyes told me to get, and Joe said: "Parm me, but I believe there is a customer before you," and he went over to wait on The Widow, too. She is never served by *only* Frank or Joe, but by *both*. The Widow is wiggling and saying: "Oh, dear, prices are so high," and Joe says: "Don't you worry about that one minute. We'll fix you up with something special. Just give us a clue." And The Widow says: "Perhaps a little rack of lamb." And Frank said: "I've got a prime spring lamb in the back I'll cut it from," and Joe says: "No, let *me* cut it." I want to tell you, when they finally put that rack of lamb on the counter The Widow could scarcely see over it and she tripped gaily away for, I think, five bucks, and Frank called after her: "Shall I help you carry it to your car?"

And I said: "I never carried off that much meat for five bucks," and Joe said, and I think this is the crux of the matter: "You are not as pretty as The Widow. Now what can I get you?"

And I said: "At the prices you charge the rest of us, I'll have to settle for half a pound of hog liver."

Mrs. McMurty came in then and she is very status conscious. She thinks your social position depends on how much you pay for things. For instance, she wears only special-order corsets, made in France at $195 each, that make her look like she is cast in concrete but give her something to make her feel better-dressed than ordinary women. So she pointed to a tray of sweetbreads in the case and Frank said: "Four sixty a pound," and Mrs. McMurty said coldly: "I did not inquire how much it cost. I will take two pounds." McMurty's going to get awfully tired of sweetbreads.

When Joe gave me my package of hog liver he said Frank clean forgot to give The Widow two big bones for Fifi, her poodle, and would I mind dropping them off at her place and I said, why, of course. They made a simply delicious soup which will keep us going until Friday. Let Fifi eat dog biscuit.

One day when I was buying a pound of fish heads for a birthday present for Lucky, my cat friend, Frank was telling me about the old days in Chicago when he learned his trade near the stockyards – that's where he got the nickname Old Featherthumb. He had the fastest thumb in the Midwest for weighting the scales. "The one place a customer should be wary in a meat market is with a short butcher," he told me in confidence. "A short butcher looks up at the scales and he has got to read them an ounce or two higher. That is, unless he stands on a box. When I have to employ a short butcher, I insist he stand on tippy-toes. On the other hand, a tall butcher looks down on the scales and reads the scale less than the actual weight, and the shop loses. Scales should be high for a tall butcher – but that means the customer would have to stand on a box. It gets complicated . . ."

* * *

You will be glad to know I have acted as a peacemaker in a nasty situation in the neighborhood, I made peace between Mrs. Fuller and Joe Nietzsche, the delicatessen man. He's quite a philosopher and enjoys a good reputation here, particularly for homemade sausage, except that he has this weakness about patting ladies when they lean over his pickle barrel. It is really an automatic thing, a conditioned reflex.

What happened, Mrs. Fuller was picking out six of the largest pickles and had her hand pretty near up to her elbow in the barrel, and Mr. Nietzsche was not strong enough to resist the opportunity presented to him, and he patted Mrs. Fuller. She was very much offended and threw some pickles around the store and walked out and said she would never go there again.

But I was able to persuade her that she was being discriminatory. I pointed out that she permits Mr. Dibble at least one pinch at any party they both attend – everyone knows that Mr. Dibble has this compulsion to pinch ladies when he has had more than two drinks, and it is the custom to allow him one pinch per lady before anybody hollers copper. I told Mrs. Fuller that if she tolerates one pinch from Mr. Dibble, who has a mind like the inside of a sofa pillow, why should she object to a pat from Mr. Nietzsche, who is one of the great minds of our time.

I guess she got the point because she was back at Mr. Nietzsche's yesterday and he seemed pleased she wasn't sore any more. But I noticed she was making *him* dive into the pickle barrel for the largest dills. I said to her as Mr. Nietzsche presented a perfect target: "Now is your chance to get even," but she chickened out.

Frank and Joe, the butchers, have branched out into the catering business in competition with Mrs. Lucretia Borgia and her husband, Cesare, who tends bar. They had a monopoly on the clam dip and casserole business around here until now. Joe Neitzsche, the delicatessen man, was going to join the Borgias, but his lawyer insisted he take out some heavy malpractice insurance, so he gave up the idea.

This was because if you hire Lucretia to cater a Saturday party, she makes the salads on Wednesday and leaves them uncovered in her kitchen. The fruit salads are not too lethal, but when she serves a jellied ham salad it is Goodbye Harry for quite a time.

Joe Oedipus, the psychiatrist's cat, attends all the neighborhood parties because he likes hors d'oeuvres, and he acts as food taster for me. I give him a spoonful, and if his tail goes straight up and he walks away after sniffing it, I won't touch it either. He is a dependable cat and his decisions are invariably right. If Joe Oedipus is at a party, I walk out happy and in good health and say polite goodnights to the hostess and Lucretia while other guests are calling ambulances.

With Frank and Joe in the catering business now, too, you won't have to worry about stopping off at the emergency ward on the way home. But you do worry about spotting your clothes. Frank and Joe have two standard dinners. One is Finger Foods Polynesian with a hula dancer (Joe puts on a grass skirt and does a very convincing hula, actually), and the other is the Henry the Eighth Dinner where you also use your fingers and just tear things to pieces and throw bones over your shoulder and drip fat on the floor. They have this barbecue in the back of their shop and prepare their catered dinners between customers during the day. At night they bring the whole meal to your house right from the barbecue. Naturally, being butchers, it is mostly meat and sets the host back pretty good. If you want hot biscuits and creamed chicken you hire Lucretia.

The Finger Food Dinner is mostly skewered meats that you can eat without ever having to put down your drink, and things to scoop on crackers. I like the Henry the Eighth dinners better, however. What happens here is that Frank and Joe bring over a whole hot roasted turkey and a spiced baked ham and roast ducks, cut up serving size, and you can walk around a party with a drumstick in one hand and a martini in the other.

* * *

Once in a while I come home from a hard day at the office and Green Eyes, with a wave of the hand, shows me four loaves of freshly baked bread. "I made bread today," she says proudly. And I say: "You mean you heated up some premixed dough." And she says, "Oh, shut up!" which is certainly no way to talk to a devoted husband.

Grandma sometimes bakes bread from scratch. It's a solid, frontier-type ranch bread. She calls it Indian bread. In the old days the settlers would give it to the Indians, and after that the Indians would stay away. It has great crust, but it is almost *all* crust. It rises only about an inch and a half. I believe she takes it out of the oven and sits on it halfway through the baking. Grandma says it is the fault of the electric stove. She thinks we should have an old-fashioned range so I can chop and bring in wood.

But she more than makes up in dumplings. They are huge and light as a baby's breath. She seems to have no recipe, but she makes allowances for temperature, barometric pressure, wind drift and the sign of the Zodiac. Sometimes I say to her: "How about some dumplings for dinner, kid?" and she looks out the window and holds a wet finger up in the air on the back porch and says: "No, it is a bad day for dumplings." It's weird.

Now Green Eyes' Aunt Bitty makes sausage at home as gifts for the rest of the family and, whenever she visits you to tell you who is dead or who is incurably ill, why she leaves you a sausage. To speed your own departure, I think.

Aunt Bitty makes her own sausages according to an Old World recipe which had been handed down from mother to daughter ever since they fled from a leper colony in the Aegean, and it is pretty much like a witch's broth, but thicker. I have a nasty suspicion they are alive, and I have, indeed, seen them move. I don't demand much of a sausage except that it lie still while I am eating it, and I have known some of Aunt Bitty's Old World sausages to move from one side of the refrigerator to the other in the course of a night. So as soon as she leaves, I always take her sausage right down to the garbage can. It is the garlic in them, I think, that vitalizes them.

Everyone I know is dieting, including me, and I can't

understand why I don't lose any weight. My diet for a typical day is a glass of tomato juice and two cups of coffee for breakfast. For lunch a cup of consomme, four ounces of roast beef and a cup of black coffee, and for dinner a small green salad, spinach and poached white fish with tea. And I am famished.

Then I watch television. Now you can't just sit and watch television. You should nibble something, and I believe it is all right as long as what you nibble has no nourishment.

I say to Green Eyes as I open a package of potato chips: "I eat like a bird these days," and she says: "Yes, like a vulture." It is cruel of her. She will say anything for a laugh. She does not know real hunger.

I can hear you exclaiming: "Everyone knows that potato chips are loaded with fats and calories!" No such thing. First of all, when potatoes are first peeled and sliced at the factory, they are floated in churning water and the starch precipitates out. What is left is mostly cellulose, and cellulose couldn't hurt anybody. Perhaps there is a drop or two of fat clinging to them as a result of being fried, but it is polyunsaturated vegetable oil and it is *good* for you.

So when the potato chips are gone, I open a package of deep-fried bacon rinds. A whole big package weighs only two and a half ounces! You see, they put this bacon rind through some process where it is exploded and all the fat is lost, and again, only cellulose remains. Of course it *is* a little salty and gives you a thirst, but I find a quart or two of fruit juice or milk will easily satisfy it.

So I eat the package of bacon rinds. So far I have eaten only cellulose since I sat down to watch television, and already I feel as if I had eaten a heavy, nourishing dinner. My spirit soars and even television begins to look good.

When you are on a strict diet as I am, balance is everything. Now nuts are heavy in protein, and protein is very desirable. I ask myself at intervals: "Have I had enough protein today?" and very often I find myself answering: "No, I have not." So I open a can of peanuts.

Now a few peanuts never hurt anyone, particularly the dry-roasted variety. That's the kind I buy and bring home. I can't get Green Eyes to stock peanuts on the emergency shelf. She says peanuts are not an emergency. I don't think she understands the importance of balance in diet.

So I eat a can of peanuts and it is a small can, and I have been very faithful on my diet, eating things that have a lot of protein and plain cellulose and few calories – and yet, the very next morning the scales show that I have lost nothing or maybe even *gained* one or two pounds. Sometimes I get so discouraged.

CHAPTER V

Looking Back

Lots of people like to dabble in genealogy, but I'll bet few of them can trace their families as far back as Green Eyes can. I mean Green Eyes' family goes all the way back to Sodom and Gomorrah, although she denies it. They ran the sightseeing buses outside the Hilton Gomorrah and the Sodom Sheraton, and their twenty-dollar late night tour was the best in the Twin Cities. It included a quick run through three gambling halls, a couple of strip and porn shows and a five-course dinner with a dinner show, "An Evening With Jack the Ripper."

People sometimes ask me: "Doesn't your wife's family get sore when you write about them?" and my answer is no, they don't, because they can't read. Green Eyes sometimes gets sore and the cooking at home falls off considerably for a few weeks, but that is what a writer must pay for freedom of expression.

But to get back to the genealogy of Green Eyes' family, it dates from Sodom and Gomorrah and was very prominent there, the absolute dregs of society. One of them, in fact, was Chief Dreg and was reelected time and time again in successive crooked elections. Green Eyes denies her family came from Sodom and Gomorrah, and she tells a ridiculous story that they came from Scotland and Germany and France, but I've seen them and I know better. You can assemble them anywhere, like in my living room, and you can clear the room in an instant merely by shouting, "Stop, thief!"

Green Eyes' folks ran the sightseeing buses in Sodom and Gomorrah and had signs up around town, "See the Twin Cities After Dark," and they advertised an economical family package, with half rates for kiddies. And for the really debauched who were looking for the absolute ultimate in action, they had gin rummy games going in both hotels. I mean they'd gin before you even saw what cards they had dealt you.

The family experiences in the Twin Cities have been passed down in legendary form from mother to daughter over the centuries, and I occasionally hear my mother-in-law mention to Green Eyes something that happened in Gomorrah as if it happened down the street only yesterday. But they break off talking when I appear, and when I ask: "What have you two got your heads together about this time?" they say, "Nothing."

I can't for the life of me figure out how any of Green Eyes' family got away when Sodom and Gomorrah were destroyed. I suppose a few of them were in distant countries promoting the tourist business when it happened. I suppose they were in Persia or Jordan or Egypt stepping out of alleys and whispering to passersby: "Hey, Bud. Innerested in a little action out of town?" Or maybe they had been deported, too depraved for even the wicked people of their home towns. When archeologists some day unearth tablets with lists of survivors of the destruction of Sodom and Gomorrah, I haven't a doubt in the world that the names of some of Green Eye's distant relatives will be found on them.

Neither Green Eyes nor I have done much work on our family trees but we do know there was a Jukes on her side and a few Kallikaks on mine. Neither of us has had to spend a cent on genealogical research because it's all there in any sociology book, family trees and all.

My own family dates from Babylon, where they were in the construction business. Among other projects they worked on was the Tower of Babel, which, unhappily, was never completed because they ran into communication problems. There are many versions of this difficulty, but I prefer to think that their workmen and mechanics came to my ancestors and asked for more money, and my family simply didn't understand what they were saying so work stopped, permanently – the longest strike in history!

Any time I mention some of Green Eyes' family she is very quick to remind me of some of the more colorful members of mine like my old Great-Uncle Charley who lived on Nantucket and whose bathroom consisted of a portable tin tub and a very small structure in the back pasture. He believed, as many of his generation did, that frequent bathing weakens a person, a belief that he impressed upon me when I was on a vacation to Nantucket as a small boy.

I've heard the family talk about Great-Uncle Charley who bathed only in the spring and the fall, after his womenfolk caught him. When they began to hint it was time for the semi-annual bath, he would disappear. By fanning out and beating the brush they often caught him. Sometimes it was necessary to have the sheriff bring out the dogs, who always went unerringly to Great-Uncle Charley, their nostrils aquiver. The same thing happened in the fall before they sewed Great-Uncle Charley into his winter woolen underwear. I mean, I come from a hardy people and it took some time for Green Eyes to convince me that Bathing Can Be Fun. After all, Great-Uncle Charley bathed twice as much as King Louis XIV of France, who bathed only *once* a year.

But Green Eyes was smart. When we married she gave me a captain's cap to wear in the tub and a big red ferryboat to sail in it and let me stay as long as I wished, making waves for the boat to toss upon, and I soon forgot all about Great-Uncle Charley until this very moment.

The only famous member of Green Eyes' current family is her Uncle Whitney who is an artist. He makes mobiles out of telephone wire he strips from poles, and we have all of us been waiting, hopefully, for the day when he would try to strip a hot power line.

Anyway, Uncle Whitney's mobiles are quite popular because they are erotic. He has had a number of exhibits in important galleries and fine critical revues in art journals and is considered to be one of the top erotic artists in the art world. I don't understand it. They don't look dirty to me, they just look like bent wire, but I guess it is what's in the mind of the artist and viewer that makes them erotic. At any rate Green Eyes' family is extremely proud of him.

Last Thanksgiving was one of the best family dinners and reunions we ever had, and Green Eyes' relatives enjoyed it hugely. As far as we know they got home safely – all except Uncle Whitney.

Uncle Whitney saw a number of people going into the McMurty house across the street, so he left our house and went across and walked right into the McMurtys' with them. I understand he is still there. He is an engaging fellow and a great martini drinker, which would make him extremely compatible with Mr. McMurty, who is no slouch in that field. As a guest Uncle Whitney poses no problem if you remember to keep him away from an open flame.

The reason he is still at the McMurtys' is (1) that the McMurtys have no immediate family in this area and Uncle Whitney, all by himself, satisfies their need for a family reunion, and (2) he took Mrs. McMurty's washing machine apart at midnight last Thursday and he probably won't have it back together again until, oh, about the end of the month. Actually, all the washer needed was a new fuse, but he thought he might as well give it a complete overhaul while he was there. He has never had training as an electrician, but after all his experience with electricity while stealing power lines to make his mobiles, he is not intimidated when dealing with only 200 volts.

The washing machine is running pretty good now except it spins in the opposite direction, which perplexes Mrs. McMurty, but she will adjust to it.

I think we had twenty-two members of Green Eyes' family and a few of mine for Thanksgiving dinner, plus some strangers who wandered in. I think during the day a transcontinental bus stopped outside our house and the passengers came in, because at one time I counted five persons standing outside the downstairs powder room and three outside the upstairs baths, and one of the persons upstairs asked me when the bus left for Scranton. It was a confusing day.

We see Green Eyes' relatives only on holidays. The rest of the year they are hiding from the police or Board of Health or bill collectors, and about all we see of them otherwise is their pictures on the post office bulletin board, full-face and profile. Grandma is the only one who remembers their names, and she stands at the front door and greets them by asking: "What name are you going under now?"

The only guest who wasn't related was The Widow. Green Eyes found out she was going to be alone on Thanksgiving and invited her. She came early to help Green Eyes and made the salad and the biscuits and mixed the punch and wouldn't let me have any until just before dinner. I introduced The Widow to the guests, and when the women asked me who she was I told them a big story, that she was an unwed mother who had kept her child and was bringing it up to regard her boy friends as father surrogates in the modern fashion. They were shocked to their shoesoles and, for once, didn't wander around the house guessing what we had paid for everything, but gathered in corners staring at The Widow with their faces working like a barrel of mash. And the women were too preoccupied with The Widow this time to steal anything, but it was at this dinner that Uncle Biff took the silver gravy boat – and it was full of gravy, too. One minute it was on the table and the next it was gone, gravy and all.

The last one who helped herself to gravy was Aunt Bitty. She is seven feet tall and wears men's oxfords but she is too thin to conceal a gravy boat, and she is not the kind. She is the only one of Green Eyes' family who brings us something every Christmas. She brings us a sack of chicken droppings for our garden from the chicken farm she and her husband, Uncle What's-His-Name, run. You can't use it on house plants or they grow big enough to strangle you when you walk by.

Year after year I go downtown on the bus the day after Christmas and the fellows say: "What did you get for Christmas, Welch?" and I say: "I got fifty pounds of chicken droppings," and they act like it is some big joke. I give Aunt Bitty credit for trying. The rest of Green Eyes' relatives come with only appetites and extra pockets sewn into their linings. It's the ones who show up with empty shopping bags, however, that scare me the most.

At home the relatives drink kerosene, but at my house when I ask them what they want to drink they invariably say Scotch. So I have this decanter which says Scotch in gold letters, and I fill it with three-dollar bourbon and the guests say it is the best Scotch they ever had.

Grandma, Green Eyes' mother, is strong for relatives. She has them scattered all over the world, they are numbered in thousands and she knows all of them intimately. She went to Europe once for four months and she ate every meal with a relative and didn't stay in a hotel room more than two nights, and each time the hotel was owned by a relative.

The only definite information I got from her about them was that she visited the Tower of London and one of her relatives was a Beefeater and the poor fellow has terrible trouble with his stomach. I asked her what she thought of the Crown Jewels and she said: "I saw those. Mr. Claymore took me through. He's Sarah's third cousin, you know. He just can't put anything solid into his stomach these days."

Of course Grandma is in her eighties and she has had time to accumulate lots of relatives – French in France, Italians in Italy, English in England, Norwegians in Norway and I don't know what. They all love her and write her letters, and I am always afraid to turn away a stranger at my front door because he could always be one of Grandma's relatives. Consequently, I am frequently caught by door-to-door salesmen.

I did turn away a fellow once and had him practically all the way out to the street by the scruff of the neck until he proved he was a passing relative. He said: "Now look here! I have a right to see Bessie, she's a Daniels." So that night he took us all out to dinner and there was so much champagne we were using it in the fingerbowls. Actually, I don't mind in the least Grandma's rich relatives. It's the poor ones who bug me.

Like the time we took Grandma to Vancouver, Canada, with us, and I hadn't even paid off the bellboy for bringing up our luggage before the rooms began to fill up with Grandma's Canadian relatives. One old lady knocked at my door – she looked as if she had just been run over by a bus – and I said: "Good heavens, an apparition!" And she said: "Is Bessie here?" And I said: "Have they announced us on radio and TV already?" And she said: "I am related to Bessie through the Claymores, you know." And I said: "How is Mr. Claymore at the

Tower of London? Is his stomach still troubling him?" And she said: "He can't put anything solid into it."

So she put her hat and coat on *my* bed, straightened her wig and marched into Grandma's room right to the afternoon tea tray with the pastries, and nineteen other relatives fell on her with glad cries.

Grandma never hesitates to ask people their names. For instance she went to a branch post office near the Vancouver hotel to get stamps for postcards to send to all the other relatives, and she asked the lady at the stamp window her name and the lady said "Philpot." You'd think that anyone with an unusual name like Philpot wouldn't have relatives running loose, but Grandma found she was related to her away back. Mrs. Philpot showed up at the hotel, too.

She came into my room while I was writing and said: "What are you doing?" And I said: "I am not going to tell you." And she said: "You talk like a Philpot. My husband is abrupt and short the way you are." And I said: "What a pity he can't be here." And she said: "Oh, he's coming. I phoned him." He did come, and he stayed a half a bottle of rye.

* * *

It is educational to trace your family back through the ages because you run across many interesting and unusual bits of history you'd never ordinarily learn. For instance, take that ancient people known as the "Mouse-eaters," who lived about two hundred miles southeast of Mexico City in 7,000 B.C. Of course, they didn't know they were living near Mexico City at the time, or even in Mexico. But that is beside the point. The point is that at some time they stopped eating mice and began to make and eat tortillas instead, and this change of diet puzzles the anthropologists who are studying them.

It doesn't puzzle me a moment. It is quite obvious what happened. The women were responsible. Somewhere along the line a woman, and then another woman, and then a whole colony of women became persuaded that eating mice was low-class business and not consistent with the culture every woman longs for. One day a fellow came home from a hard day of chasing mice and found his supper already prepared.

"What is *this?*" he asks incredulously.

And his wife says: "It's vegetables, that's what it is."

And he says: "I never heard of nobody eating vegetables. People eat mouses. Always have, always will."

And she says: "Try it, it's delicious."

And he says: "Is there a mouse in it?"

And she says: "No. It's time we had a little culture around here. I'm embarrassed to death when we travel and meet other peoples and they say, 'There go a couple of mouse-eaters.'"

And he says: "What do you call this thing?"

And she says: "It's a salad."

And he says: "Nothing doing. I want mouses."

And she says: "You see how little culture you have? You don't even know how to form the plural for mouse. It is not mouses. It is mice."

And he says: "I eat one mouse. Then I eat another mouse. I eat two mouses."

And she says: "You eat one *mouse*. You eat two *mice*."

And he says: "I never eat no mice."

And she says: "Oh, for heaven sake, go out and invent the wheel or something."

Then he went out and called to a friend and said wonderingly: "When you eat a mouse, that is one mouse. When you eat two mouses, that is one mice."

The only way this sort of confusion could be arrested was to stop eating mice and to start eating tortillas.

These people left no cave drawings to substantiate this. We can assume from the absence of cave drawings that the women were better housekeepers than most primitives. They had rules. They didn't let their kids draw on the walls on rainy days when they couldn't go out to play.

I understand the mouse-eaters began to eat avocados rather late in their development and, again, I'm certain the women were responsible for its introduction into the diet.

"We have a surprise tonight," said the first adventurous woman. "Avocados!" And the man said: "I might eat it if you put a mouse on it." And she said: "You have just regressed four thousand years. We haven't eaten mice since I don't know when."

And he said: "It might be better if you mashed it up into guacamole."

And it was her turn then to say: "What's guacamole?"

And he said: "You're the smart one. Go out and invent it."

* * *

Women really have been an ennobling influence on men — male men. I don't want you to confuse "male men" with "mailmen" or letter carriers. I put this in so that Fred, my mailman, will know that I am not writing about him. He is a hominid too, just like all the rest of us, but I would be the last to tell him. He is a very friendly fellow, but he is quick to resent anything he believes to be critical of the postal service.

Dr. Louis Leakey, the famous British anthropologist, classifies the hominids who lived about twenty-five million years ago into three groups: the near-man, Zinjanthropus; the human-like Homo Habilis; and the Pithecanthropine. Dr. Leakey thinks they probably existed side by side and maybe even intermingled at prehistoric cocktail parties, a theory other anthropologists deny.

"I want you to meet one of our new neighbors, a Pithecanthropine," Dr. Leakey thinks a hostess would say, and a Homo Habilis would reply: "I never heard of a Pithecanthropine before," and the hostess would say: "He's a relative of Java Man and Peking Man and he's a tool maker." And the new Pithecanthropine neighbor would say: "You innerested in buying a stone axe?"

There's evidence that the lower Zinjanthropus girl did often, in fact, marry the almost-human species, Homo Habilis, to improve her social position. She still cooked like a Zinjanthropus, and when you find Zinjanthropus cooking utensils together with Homo Habilis weapons – and perhaps an old pair of Homo Habilis pants – you can be certain a male Homo Habilis was eating terrible food there and wondering if a buxom Zinjanthropus figure was worth it.

"I don't want to be a low-class Zinjanthropus all my life," a girl would tell her mother. And her mother would say: "Your daddy is one of the lowest hominids possible and he's always been nice, in a stupid way." But when her daughter finally married above her station, this same mother would hurry to her sister low-hominids and happily boast: "My daughter has married a Homo Habilis, and that's not the best part. He's a doctor!"

* * *

I believe I must be some sort of human vacuum cleaner, sucking up all the odd bits of information that somehow land on my desk. Just recently I learned that Paul Revere was not only a superb silversmith and patriot and midnight rider, but was also a dentist.

Revere had a huge tooth hanging outside his shop along with his silversmith sign. You would go into his shop and he would say: "Good morning, sir. Interested in a little genuine pewter?" and you'd point to your swollen cheek and say: "No. I gob a bad toob." and he would say: "Kindly step into the rear of my shop. The screaming disturbs the other customers," and he would produce a pair of pliers and perhaps a tin-snip, and whippo, whappo! – no more tooth.

I don't know why Longfellow in his poem failed to identify Revere as a dentist. To me there is something inspirational about a dentist galloping through the night with a pocket full of dental mirrors and drills. I assume he had a pocket full of dental mirrors and drills because we know the British caught him between Lexington and Concord – and released him! It is my theory that he told them he was a dentist and was on his way to treat a bad case of malocclusion. "How do you like that," the captain of the British patrol exclaimed," a dentist who makes house calls?"

On the same night that Paul Revere and William Dawes set out for Concord, a certain Israel Bissel also set out from Boston by horse to warn the Continental Congress in the south that war had begun. Bissel's journey was far more tiring, hazardous and of greater strategic value. Longfellow might well have used him for his hero. Longfellow would say to his wife: "I have a new poem here.'Listen, my children, and you shall hear / of the midnight ride of Israel Bissel.'" And she would say: "I don't know. Somehow that second line doesn't swing. Why don't you try 'Israel Bissell / rode through thick and thistle?'"

A week later he asks her: "How about this? 'Listen, my children, and you shall hear / of the midnight ride of William Dawes.'" And she says: "But Dawes doesn't rhyme with 'hear.' Suppose you make it 'Listen, my children, and you shall hear / of the midnight ride of *Paul Revere*?'"

And he says: "But that's so obvious! A fat lot you know about poetry. Anyway, Revere was only an advertising dentist, and the British pulled him off his horse a mile or two beyond Lexington. Dawes made it all the way, and so did Dr. Sam Prescott. They rode from Lexington to Concord while the British were frisking Revere and finding his pockets full of dental mirrors and drills."

And she says: "I'd like to see you rhyme Prescott with something." And he says: "I wouldn't call him Prescott. I'd call him Dr. Sam. How about 'Listen, my children, and you, too, ma'am, / of the midnight ride of Dr. Sam?'" And she says: "That's terrible. If you use that, your poem will never become a classic."

As wives often do, she finally prevailed and I, for one, am glad she did.

Historical utterances which go ringing down through the ages should be regarded with some skepticism. They probably were never said at all.

Take John Alden and Priscilla. When he was urging her to marry Captain Smith, she is reputed to have said, coyly: "Why don't you speak for yourself, John?" I don't believe it for a minute. Those days girls weren't so bold-speaking, they got their points over in sneakier ways.

I think she said to herself: "He's cute! I wonder why he doesn't ask for a date himself." And later she said to her best friend (who promised she wouldn't tell a soul): "He's darling, and I'd rather date him than that dull Smith boy." and when this honor-bound best friend immediately told John Alden, he looked amazed and said: "Gosh, why didn't she tell me? I think she's kinda cute, too."

Then there is Henry Ford's famous remark that his customers could have any color car, "so long as it is black." Kids learn that one at their mothers' knees.

More likely that was just another apocryphal saying, uttered, actually, by Joe Apocryphal who worked in the paint shed at Mr. Ford's Dearborn plant. "Here we go again," he said, picking up his paint gun one day, "Black, black, black. Customers can have any color they want as long as it's black! This production line is killing me." And Mr. Ford was at a meeting that afternoon with his public relations and production departments, discussing the need for a new slogan to beef up sales.

"How about saying, 'The Ford car is a good car?'" Mr. Ford suggested, but the PR men said: "Excuse us Mr. Ford, sir, but it doesn't swing. We need something more gutsy." And a production man said: "Some of the boys in Research and Planning have come up with a sensational idea. How about painting some of our cars green?" And Mr. Ford said: "If we paint some green, then they won't all be black."

And the production man said: "That reminds me of something I heard in the paint shed this morning, Joe

Apocryphal was grousing about his job being monotonous and he said: 'Customers can have any color they want as long as it is black.'" And the PR men said: "That's it! But Mr. Ford, sir, ought to make the historic utterance, not Joe Apocryphal."

Mr. Ford liked it, so they made Joe Apocryphal sign a waiver to all rights to the historic utterance and they took him off the paint line and promoted him to the assembly line, mounting the hand accelerators at a dollar and a half a week raise in salary. So Mr. Ford has gone down in history with the utterance, and Joe was happy, too, with the raise that bought him an extra bucket or two of beer on Saturday night.

* * *

I sometimes wonder how history would read if the great army and navy figures of our national past had been required to have psychological as well as physical tests periodically. Surely a few of them must have been giving battle orders while they had birds sitting on their heads.

A psychiatrist who studied some of our past navy and army heroes has found evidence that they had periods of forgetfulness and aberration due, no doubt, to long, lonesome months on duty. He quotes from the life of Farragut, the American naval commander who said: "Damn the torpedoes. Full speed ahead." It seems there were days when Farragut didn't know whether it was half-past two or twenty minutes to six. "What time is it?" he would ask other officers and they would say: "It is sixteen hours, sir, four bells." And he would say: "How much is that in regular time?" And they would say: "It means four o'clock, sir," And he would say: "If it's four o'clock, why don't you say four o'clock?"

Farragut made his most memorable remark in Mobile Bay in 1864, the same year in which he retired.

"What are those things?" he asked, pointing to objects rushing through the water towards them as the fleet moved in to bombard Forts Morgan and Gaines. "Why, they are torpedoes, sir," he was told. "Well leave us ignore them and proceed at once to our objective," he ordered. And a junior officer stationed nearby, who was keeping the log said: "Would you mind rephrasing that order? In its present shape I don't think it will go ringing down through the ages."

And the admiral said: "Oh, dammit, man, I haven't time. And I can't bother about those things in the water. Tell the captain to go a little faster."

After the public relations staff back at base looked over the log, they revised the order to a pretty respectable famous quotation. Farragut, himself, approved of it, although he couldn't for the life of him recall having said anything like it or even having ever been in Mobile Bay.

Admiral Dewey, too, had lapses of memory. Dewey is the one who is credited with saying: "You may fire when ready, Gridley," to the captain of his flagship at the Battle of Manila Bay.

There is recent evidence, though, that what Dewey said, actually, was: "You may fire when ready, Smathers." And the junior officer said: "Pardon me, sir, but who is Smathers?" And Dewey said: "Smathers is the captain of this ship, of course." And the officer said: "Sir, I fear you are thinking of Smathers, the mess officer. You talked to Smathers this morning, sir, in connection with that difficulty about your eggs."

And Dewey said: "If Smathers is not the captain, who is?" And the officer told him: "Sir, our captain is Gridley." And Dewey said: "Except for the eggs, I thought Smathers was doing a first-rate job."

CHAPTER VI

Worries

I worry a lot, three or four hours a day, about a great many things. But I like to get some *variety* into my worrying. I mean, you get weary worrying about American foreign policy, and the stock market, and inflation, and if hard rock music is here to stay, and if there is something wrong with you if you don't like Samuel Beckett's plays. Pretty soon you find you are worrying in the same old rut. The wise man goes out to hunt new things to worry about.

For example, I don't want to seem an old scarehead, but there is a bill before Congress to remove the tariff on bagpipes, and I think there is a grave danger that one of these days we shall all be standing up to our hip pockets in them. The trouble is that the bagpipe has no natural enemies, only man. You bring it into a country and it begins by taking over parades, then, finally, whole sections of cities, and, eventually, the entire nation, and you can't hear yourself think.

The bill would remove the tariff on bagpipies, and they would be freely admitted after being held briefly in quarantine to insure they were not carrying rabies, or hoof and mouth disease, or any other epizootic malady.

People tell me it is silly to say that bagpipes are alive. But if you have ever been around when a piper puts one down on a table, you know for a fact that the nasty thing exhales and goes "ahhhhhhhhhh." I have seen them tremble for minutes after being put down. Occasionally, one will rise up furtively and look around. I have known them to pinch passing girls. At a party once I saw a bagpipe left on a bed going through women's purses. I slapped a bagpipe once when it was reaching for caviar on toast points on an hors d'oeuvre tray, and it squirted ink at me.

People say they are not alive. All right. Just lock up a couple of bagpipes together for six months, and you will have not only the original two bagpipes, but three or four little ones as well – providing you have made sure the original pair were male and female.

I doubt if the bagpipe can ever be truly domesticated, and I personally have seen one actually turn on its owner during a Fourth of July parade. It tried to strangle its own piper. It took three other pipers to pull the nasty thing off the unfortunate man – it had him by the throat – and it required a policeman's bullet to dispatch it as it lay threshing in the street after five musicians and part of the crowd had failed to subdue it by jumping on it. All this time the other bagpipes in the band looked on indifferently. Thank heaven they are self-contained creatures and seem to have no tribal organization.

I saw another incident in which a bagpipe, in a moment of unexplained hostility – perhaps the piper's hands were cold – backfired and tried to blow up the piper and very nearly succeeded.

Frisby, of Cornell, relates various experiments to interbreed bagpipes and octopi and says at least one attempt was successful. The "octobag" had suckers on its reeds, and the bag emitted the ink which an octopus characteristically discharges when attacking or retreating from the enemy. Before this creature could be connected up with an air hose to sound its A, it climbed up the laboratory wall and through a skylight and was tracked as far as Fall Creek Gorge, where its progress downstream was accompanied by a progression of bubbles. It was obviously playing something, and, under twenty feet of water, it may have sounded good.

All other efforts to mate an octopus and bagpipe have

failed as far as I can determine, although biologists are still investigating a story from Fiji concerning a bagpipe which leaped overboard from its piper's arms and took up with a squid. The two were frequently seen by native boatmen the story goes, in affectionate embrace.

In urging that the tariff be removed and the bars let down to the entry of more bagpipes into the United States, one congressman cited the fact that bagpipes are not indigenous to Scotland, or to Ireland (where they also roam in the wild state). He said that they originated in Babylonia and were known in Rome at the time of Nero.

The Roman legions carried them first into England from whence they spread by crawling over the land and swimming the Irish Sea to Scotland and Ireland. The tootling of bagpipes frightened the early Britons out of their minds. They conceived them to be evil spirits in torment, which is as good a description as any. The music made the Roman conquest of Britain that much easier.

There is reason to believe that when Rome burned, Nero wasn't playing a fiddle but was blowing an early version of the bagpipe. It was called the *tibia utricularis* and had no drone ground bass, which is the part of today's bagpipe that moans continuously. Nero played only tenor notes, tweedledee, tweedledee and like that, although on great occasions he had other pipers play dee while he played tweedle.

There is also a legend that bagpipes were turned loose on Christians in early Rome, a fate much worse than lions. Romans learned to tune bagpipes, although nobody much cared whether they were in tune or not provided they kept their distance. I've seen modern pipers tune their pipes and it is not very precise. One of the band sounds an A and the others wrestle with their instruments to an approximation, but it is uphill all the way.

You can understand why I am worried about Congress removing the tariff and exposing this nation to a new infestation. There is only one way to combat an attacking bagpipe. Stuff the reeds with corks. That smothers them. It is no good to slash the bags with knives. They heal too rapidly.

* * *

Now here's something we can all worry about pretty good. The National Cash Register Company some time ago perfected a process by which the whole of the Encyclopaedia Britannica can be reduced to a handful of little cards you can carry around in a vest pocket. The King James version of the Bible was reduced to one card only two inches square! I am not sure how you read it; you may have to call in an eagle. On the other hand, you can feed it into some machine which projects it, page by page, ten feet square on your living room wall. You can see what wonderful material there is here for the dedicated worrying man.

It is said that each page of this Bible is no larger than a paramecium, a one-celled animal that biology students peer at through microscopes in Biology I. A modern novel of, say, three hundred pages could be reduced to not much larger than a virus, and I am not sure but what most modern novels wouldn't be better that way.

But what happens to the author of the future who sits down at his typewriter knowing that his work will be reduced to the size of the germ that causes the common cold? Will he be able to write Great Themes? Will he write about characters Larger than Life? Will he write Sagas about Limitless Prairies? I think not. I'm afraid he will begin to Think Small.

As a boy I did a great deal of fugitive art around my town and I learned one thing: you have to suit the message to the medium. I worked with chalk on brick and cement walls, and I soon learned to tailor my message – my story – to the size of the wall. On large walls I could expand a theme, say things like: "John loves Mary, but Mary doesn't love John because Mary loves Bob." This is a terrifically moving triangle story situation. I mean, people would read it on the wall and go down the street saying to themselves: "John loves Mary, but Mary loves Bob. Does John know that Mary loves Bob? Is Mary the kind of girl who keeps fellows dangling?"

But if I had a very small piece of wall to work on, the best I could do was "John Mary" with perhaps a connecting heart. I was forced, because I was thinking small, to leave Bob out, the best part of the whole story. And people would go down the street saying: "John and Mary have something going. So what?"

I used to do exposés, too, on a magnificent scale, on really big walls or block-long fences. I would write: "Mr. Whitney Is A Dirty Fink." Mr. Whitney was my principal. In later years I came to realize he was not a fink at all, but an understanding, excellent teacher and administrator. But in *those days* I thought he was a fink. One could not do justice to this kind of theme on a lamp post. It took *space*.

I fear the authors of the future will write about little people doing unimportant things in rather a hurry when they realize the whole thing will be reduced to a paramecium. "I was reading one of your books the other night on a paramecium," a reader will tell an author. "What did you think of it?" the author will ask and the reader will reply: "Well, to tell you the truth, I wandered over into another book on the same film, the Complete Works of Joseph Conrad, in fact, and compared to Conrad you really smell up the joint."

Imagine trying to sell an encyclopedia, all on a four by six card. How can you get five hundred dollars for that, in easy monthly installments? They won't get me. I have an encyclopedia already. I bought it in 1942 and I am still only on Book 12, Hydroz to Jerem. I believe that when you buy an encyclopedia you should read it all the way through to get your money's worth. A lot of it is dull, but some of it is pretty good stuff to repeat on social occasions.

One night I stopped a lady cold when she came up to me asking for a light by saying: "By the way, did you know that Karl Gustav Jacob Jacobi was a German mathematician and is noted for his analysis of fractions? He investigated elliptic functions?" And her answer was interesting, I think. She said: "What are you, some kind of a creep?" But at least I made an impression on her, I saw her pointing me out to others all the rest of the evening. Now, if I had to go to all the trouble of setting up a projector to project the encyclopedia page on a wall, would I have ever learned about Professor Jacobi?

* * *

The other day I met a prominent guano salesman, and you know what he was worried about? He was worried that some day a machine would take his job! I reassured him. "A machine may audit your accounts and send out your billing, but, with *your* product, it takes a *man* to go out there and put his shoulder to the wheel and really sell it."

Many people, authors of science fiction and movie script writers, foresee the day when machines and men will be arrayed against one another for possession of the earth. Quite possibly, but one word of cheer. When that day comes, you'll find the intellectual machines – the computers and like that – whimpering in the corner. Intellectuals may start insurrections, but history tells us that intellectuals don't do the actual fighting. They're too smart. And we won't be fighting the computers. We'll be fighting gum machines and parking meters and coin boxes and big, clumsy tractors with no brains at all, just brawn. These are the machines to worry about.

When the revolution comes it could very well be led by the sullen, dark-green gum machine at my bus stop. This machine's hostility toward human beings is notorious. You put in a penny and sometimes you get gum and sometimes you don't. And if you put your finger in the return slot to get your penny back, there is a steel wedge which comes down and pinches it.

Personally, I have given up all dealings with purveying machines. I asked myself whether I wanted to be free and I answered, "Yes, I do." When you patronize one machine, you patronize them all, so now I don't even put money in parking meters any more. I drive around until I find one with unexpended time. I should help a machine hold its job! Let the machine support me!

A lot of people are worried about being replaced one of these days by computers or machines, and rightfully, I believe.

I don't know much about computer science but I do know something about food-dispensing machines and I assume they are about the same.

There is this big food-dispensing machine at my office. I give it a good sound kick every time I pass it, and it spews hot coffee on me every time it can, too, so we both know how we feel about one another. I put fifteen cents in it two years ago and no chocolate milk came out, and it wouldn't give up the fifteen cents, either. So now I have it pretty well battered on one side by kicking it every day or so. It has this big, central, bloodshot eye which follows me around the room, and when I approach you can hear the hot coffee gurgling, ready to be squirted on me, but the effective range is only five feet and easy to avoid, and the way I kick it is I approach from the side.

We have a computer in our office, too, but it doesn't know the anwer to questions it hasn't been programmed for. I mean, you ask it: "How do you feel about girls?" it just stands silent or it slowly prints out: "What is a girl?" I am certainly not going to be impressed by a machine which doesn't even know what a girl is.

Some business executives say that the reason computers are replacing people is that computers don't take coffee breaks or sick leaves. When a computer breaks down, six or seven mechanics swarm over it and have it back on the job in a few hours. But when a human employee breaks down, all you know is that his wife calls the office every other day and says: "Henry really is notfeeling well yet." Chances are Henry is as healthy as you are and is sitting around the house reading girlie magazines and watching ball games on TV.

One executive complained that people take advantage of the coffee break, that many workers don't eat breakfast at home but wait for the morning coffee break. Some bosses walk through the office at coffee time and find that employees are not only drinking coffee but also are eating Danish or doughnuts or sitting there with a piece of ham and two eggs over light. And he says that some employees devote their *whole* lunch hour to errands and shopping, and eat lunch on the afternoon coffee break! It sure plays hob with their meal schedules. And it also encourages the boss to put in computers.

This doesn't scare me much. I have been thinking about it and it should be reasonably easy, I think, for human employees to program a computer so that it would take coffee breaks and sick leaves on the final day of the World Series.

"How much is two and two?" the boss will then ask a computer and it will print out: "Sorry. Come back in about half an hour. Us machines are taking our morning break."

* * *

Sometimes I spend time worrying about great inventions and engineering problems and like that. For instance, how can engineers be sure, when driving tunnels from two opposite sides of a mountain, that the bores will meet? Traditionally, they always come within an inch or two of connecting exactly. But how can they be certain? I sometimes worry about that.

I suppose a really good engineer stands at the base of a mountain and says: "We'll start driving the tunnel, oh, I guess somewhere about here, Clyde, and then tomorrow I'll go around the mountain and start the other crew drilling somewhere on that side." And the assistant engineer says: "Chief, you pointed in the direction you want, but I wonder if that is quite definite enough. Could I ask you to maybe put a chalk mark on the mountain or something?"

And the chief says: "I'm going to leave it to you, Clyde. I believe in letting my subordinates have plenty of latitude. It developes their initiative."

The assistant chief says: "How do you want it? Straight, or should I put some curves in it, or up or down, or what?" And the Chief says: "All I care about is that the two bores meet someplace."

And the assistant chief says: "Well, suppose Charlie on his side puts in some curves and I put in some curves, we're liable to pass one another in the middle of the mountain." And the chief says: "You might come to some understanding with Charlie. Tell you what. Why don't you meet Charlie in town every Saturday night over a beer and tell one another where you are?"

This is no doubt how the famous Spiral Tunnels on the Canadian Pacific Railroad, between Hector and Field, British Columbia, came into being. The railroad clings to some ridiculous story that it was planned that way. But who ever heard of a train going into a mountain at one level and coming out at the same place a little higher up? I'm sure there was confusion and indignation at C.P.R. headquarters in Montreal when word came that the tunnel crew had described a complete circle and then come out right above where they had started!

Away back in 1888, when the Northern Pacific Railroad put the Stampede Tunnel through the Cascade Mountains, the center lines were only one inch off when they met. And you can bet the engineers took all the credit for it. Years later, when the Great Northern Railway drove an even longer tunnel through the same range, it claimed the bores met within one quarter of an inch! The Northern Pacific was understandably furious and spread a nasty rumor that the Great Northern had been able to beat the N.P. record only by employing a big crew of water witches and dowsers with divining rods who spent the entire construction time on the mountain above the bores, directing the tunneling crews below. There was even gossip that a number of the water witches lost their lives in avalanches, winter mountain blizzards and nasty encounters with bears, and that these vital statistics were never revealed to the public, not even on historic monuments.

CHAPTER VII

Art and Sex and Science

We give Art a pretty good play in our peculiar – I like to call it "typically American" – neighborhood. We have this big Art Show each year in the village at Legion Hall. Actually, the Hall is too small to contain it now, and the show spreads out all around the village square. It isn't that the Hall has grown too small, but that Art these days has grown bigger.

The Art Committee had a big hassle going this year with Hixly, my neighbor across the street. He entered a portrait of ex-President Nixon and it was very good, indeed, but it had faint numbers on it. The committee told Hixly that they couldn't take a picture that might stir up a political confrontation, especially a kit picture, painted by numbers.

The committee said last year they had forty-two pictures of Presidents submitted, all kit portraits drawn on numbered canvases, so they threw them out for this show, although they still took sailing ships because sailing ships are non-controversial.

When Hixly was turned down on Nixon, he wanted to display some of his hotel soap collection, which he has collected from all over the world, and the committee said it was an Art Show not a Hobby Show, but if Hixly wanted to make a montage or something artistic of his soap collection, they would consider it. So he made a mobile and hung some hotel soap from it, and he put an old fashioned washbasin under it, and we were all excited because we felt it was significant modern art. It goes to show how, with a little encouragement, a person can be turned away from derivative art to truly innovative art.

Mrs. Fumbles, the neighborhood's only real artist, did a four-sided portrait of Joe Nietzsche, who runs the village delicatessen. Mrs. Fumbles never paints just full-face or profile in portraits. She believes it is the artist's obligation to present a fully rounded picture, showing all sides of the head. She says if DaVinci had painted both the back and front of Mona Lisa we could have seen over her shoulder what amused her, maybe a couple of jokers in baggy pants were taking pratfalls to entertain her while she sat still.

The judges for the Art Show didn't notice the little man that Mrs. Fumbles painted off to one side of her portrait. I asked her what the little man represented, and she said it was Joe Neitzsche's "soul." I thought it was a delightful whimsy, but Dr. Spook, our psychiatrist, took a more serious view. He held that Mrs. Fumbles borrowed a technique from the ancients who were preoccupied with souls and often drew a soul beside a figure to assure the viewer that the person depicted did 'in truth' have a soul, and that Mrs. Fumbles' use of it indicated an atavistic tendency. It is his view that Mrs. Fumbles' deplorable lack of physical and muscular coordination, her dropping of dishes and forgetting to shut auto doors when she drives, is her way of getting release from tensions caused by subconscious primitive conflicts. Anyhow, Mrs. Fumbles won first award in oils.

There was one piece of sculpture which I thought was of very nearly professional quality, and it won second award in that category. It was done by the Fullers' oldest boy and consisted of an old flush tank with chain, suspended on a steel pole over a fountain made of an automobile wheel, an enameled washbasin and a pile of rusted beer cans. You pulled the chain on the flush tank and the fountain flowed up through the beer cans into the washbasin, and then a pump returned the water to the tank for the next pull. It was a terribly popular entry – you could hear it flushing during the entire time of the show and well into the following coffee hour.

I thought the judges were a bunch of nit-pickers. For instance, they gave Mr. Hixly only an honorary mention for his mobile. They complained that his soaps just hung there motionless, never moved. But he had a bar from The Parker House, Boston, circa 1923; and a Hotel Benson, Portland, Oregon, 1939; and a Physicians' and Surgeons' Soap from the St. Francis, San Francisco, 1955; and a whole bunch of other bars of really museum quality. I don't think Hixly will go to the trouble to enter the Art Show again and I don't blame him.

Mrs. Fuller did a remarkable sailing ship in house paint on a piece of veneer, with a mountain in the background and waves as regular as the teeth of an eleven-point saw. It was interesting and different, I thought, because it had only two dimensions and no perspective. It had sort of an ancient Egyptian look, but the best she got was an honorable mention.

In the Abstract Painting category, the Blairs' oldest girl submitted a blue canvas on which she painted a single horizontal yellow line, but the judges didn't give it an award because they said it was too traditional and representational. The Blairs were pretty sore about it and exhibited it later beside their auto, just outside the perimeter of the outdoor show. I saw it and agreed it was very representational – the best horizontal yellow line I ever saw on a solid blue background.

The first prize in watercolors went to Mr. Bazetti. It was the head of a trout wearing glasses and smoking a pipe. I considered it a little "cute," and the committee's first objection was that Bazetti hadn't shown the whole fish. He explained that the paper wasn't big enough, so they awarded it because there was no other watercolor entered.

It was a hot day, and Mr. Piedmont, our retired navy chief who had collected a gallery of tattoos while in service, came to

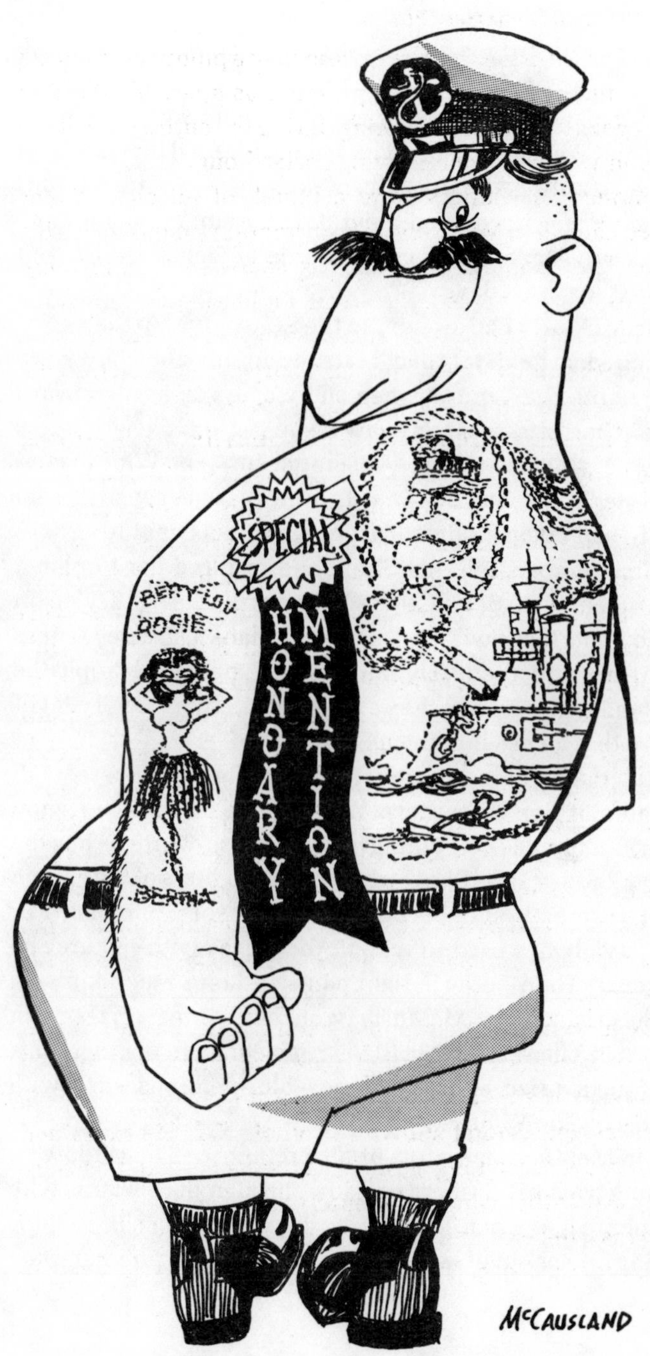
SPECIAL
HONOARY
MENTION
BETTY-LOU
ROSIE
BERTHA
McCAUSLAND

see the show in just his running shorts, and the judges saw the graphic tattoo on his back of Admiral Dewey at the Battle of Manila Bay, with Spanish ships sinking below the top of his shorts, and they went mad about it and awarded him a special honorary mention. He was so surprised and pleased to have his art finally recognized that he put the blue ribbon on his back with adhesive tape, and his wife couldn't persuade him to put on a shirt for three days.

Mr. McMurty had an entry in the Conceptual Art category. He framed a neatly typed instruction for the viewer to conceive of: The Widow when she was using her backyard sauna. When Mrs. McMurty saw it she started to tear it down until Mr. McMurty promised to scratch out "The Widow" and substitute "A Person." But he was pretty sore because he said his wife had taken all the pleasure out of his Great Idea.

Mrs. Fumbles said the Show had inspired her to plan a show of her own for next Fall. She will call it "Dylan in Ireland" and there will be a series of blank canvases before which she will recite Dylan Thomas' poems. I hope the neighbors will go to her show. We should support every bit of Culture that comes into the neighborhood.

As a matter of fact, we put together a hobby show last fall and called it The Culturama. We had it in the village Legion Hall and combined everything into one big show, including the Annual Photography Show which the Daughters of the Frozen North formerly sponsored. They got sore because Mr. McMurty always used to win all the prizes with pictures he sneaked of The Widow in tight pants and tops and bikinis. In the Culturama, Mr. McMurty won only three prizes with pictures of The Widow. Mr. Blair, a newcomer in photography, won fourth prize and two honorable mentions, also with pictures of The Widow.

Mr. McMurty gets most of his pictures of The Widow by shooting from his upstairs window through the curtains with a telephoto lens when The Widow is gardening or sun-bathing or going into or out of her sauna. He is a capable photographer and a serious one, and it doesn't help him a bit when his wife throws open the kitchen window downstairs and hollers at The Widow: "You better cover up. The old goat is upstairs making pictures of you again!"

The picture that brought McMurty first prize and Best of Show was of The Widow combing her hair in the sunshine. He titled it "Pure Gold," and her hair does seem pure gold the way he caught the sunlight streaming through it, but you ought to have seen the wives around here peering at the enlargement trying to see the color of the roots. Mrs. McMurty, who is ordinarily a lady, uttered a very unladylike remark when she first saw the picture and its title. "Pure Gold," she said loudly, "in a pig's eye!" Mrs. McMurty can't be objective about The Widow.

Blair's pictures of The Widow are technically inferior, owing to the fact that he made them with an old, four-dollar box camera with a plastic lens, but artistically they are superb. What he did was follow The Widow around one Sunday morning when she was visiting with all the neighborhood fellows who were working in their yards. She was dressed in a skimpy tennis dress and a big, floppy straw hat. As she frequently does, she slipped her arm into the arm of every fellow she talked with, a sisterly habit. Mr. Blair submitted a series of panels showing her talking to me, to Hixly, to Fuller, to Mr. Jack, to Honest Al Carter and to Mr. Piedmont, whose Battle of Manila Bay tattooed on his back was visible with the Spanish ships sinking below his belt line. Mr. Blair had maneuvered around to catch Mr. Piedmont's back and The Widow in profile and a wonderful additional touch – which I doubt he was aware of – Mrs. Piedmont could be faintly seen spying through her window curtains. Blair entitled this panel "Sister to the Whole Wide World," and, personally, I think he should have copped first prize, if not for the pictures at least for the title.

In the junior section, one of Starbright's little sons won first prize, also with a picture of The Widow, and from the angle he took the shot we are beginning to wonder if he is really only eleven. The women are pretty sore that pictures of The Widow won so many prizes, and there was some loose talk that The Widow is corrupting the men of the neighborhood, but Mrs. Fumbles told them they were showing their provincialism and she put a stop to it.

Mrs. Fumbles brought a new art form to the show which I found terribly significant, but the women thought it a lot of nonsense. She produced a tape of the sounds of a woman washing the dishes – herself, actually – and you can hear her scraping the dishes into the disposal, rinsing them under the water and putting them into the dishwasher. There is the clink of silverware and the occasional dropping and breaking of a dish in the sink, Mrs. Fumbles being poorly coordinated. Mr. Fumbles says the breakage around his home is about 216 per cent per annum.

I thought the tape, played continuously at the Culturama, was fascinating, but the women said they don't dress up and leave home to listen to somebody wash dishes.

Mr. Dibble exhibited a small totem pole he carved with his electric drill. He said it was a dirty totem pole, but I couldn't see that it was dirty. The characters on the pole all had their feet in one another's faces. That's not dirty, it's just painful. As usual, Dibble also entered one of his wooden screens depicting a nude lady with grossly exaggerated development. He has been making wooden screens and room-dividers out of plywood ever since Mrs. Dibble bought him an electric drill. All he does is drill holes to produce images when you put a light behind them. When some of the committee saw his entry this year they discussed for a time limiting it to adult viewers only. Dr. Spook says that Mr. Dibble's exaggeration of the female figures tells him quite clearly that Mr. Dibble was weaned too soon when a baby.

Mr. Piedmont was so pleased with the honorable mention he won at the Art Show for his Admiral Dewey at the Battle of

Manila Bay tattoo, that he entered his new tatoo in the Culturama. He has just about the finest tattoos in the world today. In summer, when he is mowing his lawn with his shirt off, the sightseeing bus detours down his street so the tourists can see him. He is a friendly fellow, and he will stand obligingly any length of time while the crowd is making color pictures. Besides Admiral Dewey on his back, on his chest and stomach he has "Mother" and "Home Sweet Home" and clasped hands and a lot of girl's names with a line through them. When he broke up with a girl he would have a line tattooed through her name. He also had a line drawn through "Mother," which he now regrets, but he explains it happened when he went through adolescent rebellion. He has dancing girls on both forearms, and he can make them wiggle pretty good. After he moved to our neighborhood and his wife joined the ladies' clubs, she began to object to the dancing girls because they had on even less than bikinis, and they embarrassed Mrs. Piedmont when her new lady friends saw them during the summer. So she recently persuaded him to have hula skirts tattooed on the dancing girls, and now the ladies around here think they are darling, and those are the new tattoos he entered in the Culturama. Being the lone tattoo exhibitor in art shows, Mr. Piedmont now has about eleven ribbons framed over his mantle. I tell you this to prove we *do* have culture around here.

Mr. Piedmont might have been more practical when he was picking subjects for his tattoos. I think it would be very convenient to have my bank account and cash-machine number tattooed somewhere accessible on my body, as well as my social security and safe deposit box number. Those are the numbers I am always forgetting. The other day I didn't have my checkbook and forgot my cash-machine number and, when I went into the bank, the bank officer wasn't much help. "Can't I just use any number to tide me over," I asked, "how about 34-666-803-10? That's a nice number." And he said: "Oh, for heaven sake, tell me how much you need and I'll personally lend it to you until tomorrow." It's a friendly bank, but how much less complicated it would have been if I'd had my numbers tattooed on my stomach.

Mrs. McMurty entered some of her rubbings in the Culturama. I guess you know what rubbings are. People transfer impressions from old tombstones or monuments by putting a piece of paper over the stone and then rubbing crayon or soft pencil or something over the surface. Then they frame them and hang them in their homes. It is terribly artistic and it gives the rubbers something to do when they are traveling besides listening to tour guides.

I rather admire Mrs. McMurty's rubbings because they are undeniably common and local; she gets her art without traveling very far. Her rubbings are made of signs like "Men's Room" and "No Peddlers." She hangs them in her family room.

Mrs. McMurty got her start in this hobby a few years back when her husband retired as chairman of the board of the bank. She pictured him, after retirement, as never going back to the bank and, perhaps, never going downtown again. In this she was mistaken. He still drops into the bank every morning to count a little money – and they still let him foreclose a mortgage or two. Then he lunches at the club and plays dominoes until mid-afternoon.

Well, before she realized her husband had no intention of remaining at home and helping with the housework after retirement, Mrs. McMurty made a rubbing of a number of the bank's raised-letter signs that would recall to her husband his steady rise from the ranks: "Vice President," "President," "Chairman," "Please Remove Your Hat When Talking To A Loan Officer," and like that.

Mr. McMurty's bank is a high-class bank and has raised-letter signs at the entrance to the Executive Washroom. One says: "Executive Washroom – Gentlemen Only." But another sign under it says: "Or By Invitation," which allows for a guest or lesser official on occasion. She hasn't yet made a rubbing of the newest sign in the bank, "Executive Powder Room – Ladies

Only." She plans to get one of that shortly and hang it right over Mr. McMurty's favorite chair.

Mrs. McMurty framed and fastened the "Executive Washroom" sign outside the bathroom adjoining their family room, and she got a gold plated key for Mr. McMurty to use. I think it was a sweet thing for her to do and a charming idea.

But Mr. McMurty told her: "You don't understand. There's no fun going into an executive washroom unless you know there are other people not permitted to be there." And Mrs. McMurty said: "How would it be if you barred me from going there?" And he said: "It's not enough to have just one person barred. You feel a sense of achievement only when you know that *lots* of people can't go in there."

All of that got Mrs. McMurty started on rubbings, and at the Culturama she won an award for originality with a collage of small rubbings she made of household utensils – the makers' names from her old iron food grinder, imprints from the backs of sterling silver flatware, and the bottoms of ceramic pots and like that. Mr. McMurty said it kept her busy and off his back for weeks.

* * *

I got to wondering the other night who first got the idea to put a clock in a lady's abdomen. Oh, you know what I mean. You've seen those French clocks in antique stores where the lady is a porcelain statuette and she has no clothes on and is in some classic pose and has a clock in her abdomen. When you want to know the time you look at her belly.

That idea had to start somewhere with somebody, and I can imagine it was pretty hard to sell, too. The inventor would walk into the office of the president of a big French clock company and say: "I have this idea, sir, where we have a nice statuette of a lady in the nude and we put a clock in her abdomen." And the president would say: "Do you have these headaches often?"

My old friend and neighbor Professor Carstairs tells me there is actually a case on record of a woman who had a clock in her abdomen. About 1810, he said, a young woman responded to a call for a model for a sculptor in Paris. The sculptor had been commissioned to do Diana, Goddess of the Hunt, in the nude, and he waved the young model to a screen in his studio and asked her to disrobe. When she reappeared she was carrying a scarf loosely about her midriff – and it concealed this clock.

The sculptor said: "I pay a franc an hour, and you are to keep track of the time. I'm not sure what time it is now." And the model glanced down behind the scarf and said: "It's seventeen of two."

A little later, after the sculptor's wife came in, the artist found it necessary to ask the model to remove the scarf and she did so with pretty confusion, disclosing the clock and saying: "I always find it hard to explain this, but when I was a small child I fell from a great height out of a loft onto mama's bureau and the clock." And the sculptor's wife exclaimed: "Why, good heavens, dear, you're eleven minutes fast!"

I find it difficult to believe Professor Carstairs' account, but he assures me that the sculptor was a representational artist and faithfully depicted the model, and his work was enthusiastically received, with the clock in the abdomen. The critics hailed it as having a new fourth dimension – time, and, as often happens, the clock-makers brazenly copied this original work of art for their purposes.

I believe this is as good an explanation as any. I have seen French clocks, also, protruding from the rib cages of prancing horses, but I like the lady clocks better. I think most everyone does.

* * *

I've been reading where some Episcopal chaplain at an American university says that Sex is Dead. Just like that. Sex in America is dead! To be sure, he concedes there is still some fooling around here and there, but old-fashioned sexuality has become a rarity.

I've been thinking about this a good deal. I don't often sit at my desk and think about sex because it is terribly wearing on the moral fiber, and I don't get paid enough to do that sort of thinking. But this time I made an exception and Green Eyes walked in and said: "What is the reason for that big stupid expression?" and I said: "I am thinking about Sex in Our Times," and she said: "Well, hello there, sailor! How long you going to be around town?" and I said: "You misunderstand. I am thinking about sex in an abstract, social, contemporary way."

I told her about this Episcopal priest and she said: "I have a strong suspicion that sex isn't dead. That it just phases out bit by bit as one grows older." She missed the point entirely. What I was wondering about was if an Episcopal priest is really qualified to speak on the subject of sex. I am an Episcopalian myself, and we Episcopalians have always looked down our noses at sex. I was brought up in the Episcopal church and I can't ever remember an Episcopal minister fulminating against sex in his pulpit. We Episcopalians have been all too willing to leave sex to the lesser denominations.

Some of the lesser denominations have an exciting time, I suppose, denouncing fallen men and women, but we Episcopalians accept fallen men and women as an integral part of any viable economy. We don't recognize Sin either. I don't think I have ever met a bonfide sinner in an Episcopal church. We talk about sin, but we don't expect to encounter it. Sin is for outsiders.

This Episcopal priest I read about says his observation is that certain primitive and sordid contacts may still continue among the young today, but that the libido that Freud discovered has vanished. In its place has come a kind of sex curiosity. He finds asexuality – meaning lack of sex – in the shapeless, unfeminine modern fashions, long hair for both sexes and frilly, fancy clothes men have adopted, as well as in dancing where partners significantly don't touch.

I am looking out my window right now and I see the Blair girl going down the street followed by three boys. It is hard at this distance to make out which is the Blair girl, but there is a clue. Her hair is shorter. Something draws the three boys to the Blair girl and I suspect it is some kind of sexual attraction. The boys are roughhousing with one another – but not with her. In their somewhat loutish and clumsy way they are deferring to her, and she is laughing a good deal and tossing her head and glancing at them in succession with sidelong looks. I think these young people would be amazed if you told them there was no sex in America today.

The Episcopal priest hasn't really thought through the subject of Sex Today. My own observation leads me to believe that when you turn a healthy, vigorous thing like sexuality and libidos over to a younger crowd, they instinctively know just what to do with it to keep it alive and well.

* * *

All the wives in this peculiar neighborhood of mine have extrasensory perception to a remarkable degree, and I would be glad to introduce them to any scientific groups studying the phenomenon. I have written to the Parapsychology Laboratory at Duke University about Mrs. Fuller and Mrs. McMurty, and I expect they will move in a team here almost any time soon to study both of these ladies. You know what parapsychology is, the study of psychic stuff such as clairvoyance, telepathy, extrasensory perception and why wives know instinctively what husbands are thinking and doing even when they are not present.

This sort of thing just happened to me a little while ago and it was frightening. I was sitting upstairs in my study writing and thinking it was only an hour until I could have a predinner cocktail. And Green Eyes shouted up the stairs: "There will be no drink for you tonight, my handsome prince, because you had a drink at lunch, remember?" Of course I don't remember. There is no profit in remembering things of that sort. But I submit, when a wife keeps track of her husband's drinks – one stinking little martini at lunch – it is telepathy in its most noxious form.

I have read a good deal about parapsychological research because I have been trying to understand why nature endowed wives with this fantastic understanding of husbands and why husbands don't have it. Duke University has never mentioned this aspect, not word Number One from them about how a wife can read a husband's mind clear across a city.

A friend tells me an experience of his which is right to the point. He was in his office thinking strictly business when the phone range and a voice said: "Harry, this is the Malamute Saloon and a bunch of us boys are whooping it up. Why don't you drop by on the way home?" My friend said: "I just might do that." Not more than a minute later his wife called and said: "Don't forget, dear, you are expected home early tonight." And he said: "Why?" And she said: "I don't know, but I'll think up a good reason by the time you get here." Was this extrasensory perception? I have a feeling it is what we loosely call "woman's intuition" but which is actually a much wider and more ominous power.

Mrs. Fuller can really read Fuller's mind – but not any better than all the neighborhood wives do their own husbands'. Mr. Fuller drinks too much beer and sometimes, when he and Mrs. Fuller are watching television, he will say to himself: "During the next commercial I will tell her I am going to look at the furnace and I will sneak a can of beer from the refrigerator on the way to the basement." Now he has not said anything, but when he gets up and announces: "I am going to look at the furnace," she immediately says: "Don't you take any more beer from the refrigerator because I have it counted." And he says: "Like I told you, I am going to look at the furnace." And she says: "Do you have any beer hidden in the basement?" And he says: "Certainly not!" (He has it hidden in the garage.) And she says: "Then it is probably in the garage."

* * *

Pavlov, the Russian physiologist, is my favorite scientist. He is known principally for conditioning dogs to salivate when bells are rung. But all the modern textbooks have got it the wrong way around. They tell you that Pavlov rang a bell and then a dog's mouth watered. But that wasn't it at all. The dog's mouth watered *first* and *then* he conditioned a bell to ring. This is harder to do, to be sure, but the difficulty is the true measure of his achievement.

Pavlov came to his superiors one notable day and said: "My experiments are a success. I have finally conditioned a bell to ring whenever a dog's mouth waters." And they told him: "Pavlov, you've been working hard and look tired. Isn't it possible you have this reversed? Think about it a moment, Haven't you conditioned the *dog* instead of the bell? Doesn't the bell ring first and then the *dog's* mouth waters?"

And Pavlov looked them right in the eye and said: "Not at all. I will leave the bell here with you and I will take the dog outside and make his mouth water and the bell will ring." And about five minutes later the bell began ringing and they looked out the window and Pavlov was teasing the dog with a chopped liver sandwich from his own lunch.

One of the superiors said: "Gentlemen, it is well and good to make awesome scientific discoveries like this but we must think of the public good. Isn't it best for the layman to believe that first the bell rings and then the dog's mouth waters?"

And that's the way it went out in the news release and Pavlov died a broken man because the enormity of his discovery was never truly disclosed.

* * *

I wonder, sometimes, about expressions people commonly use. Such as "to go back and forth." When you think about it, you must go forth before you go back, so, over the years the figure of speech got turned around. Somewhat the same thing happened to the term, "put the cart before the horse." I suppose that has something to do with physics, that a horse can pull better than push. But away back in history some man probably did put a cart before a horse.

Only recently Professor Preston Carstairs, my friend, the behaviorist psychologist and part-time tea-leaf reader at the Mother Earth Tearoom, told me my suspicions were true. The Professor is articulate in all fields of learning and recalled that in 1784 a young man, Hans, in Rotterdam, Holland, went to his employer, a cheese jobber whose carts went out into the countryside to pick up Gouda and Edam cheeses, and told him that he believed a horse behind a cart could actually push more cheese than the same horse in front of the cart could pull.

"It is a matter," young Hans said, "of persuading the horse to forget all the programming he has previously received. Once you've taught him to turn to the right to make the cart swing left, and to turn left to make it swing right, the thing is done."

The employer immediately said: "Well, if you're so smart, where will the driver sit when the horse is behind the cart? Who's going to be up front to direct traffic?" And Young Hans replied: "That's the only part of the problem I haven't licked yet."

And the employer said: "Believe me, with the cheese business the way it is, I can't afford two men on a cart, so where's the saving? Besides even if you do work out some system it's still no good. People have always said you can't put the cart before the horse, and you'd better not try to fly in the face of tradition."

But Hans experimented and he found that if the cart were highly loaded with cheese, the horse behind couldn't see over it and wouldn't move. He discovered horses are more interested in where they are going than in where they've been. This discovery is widely known in the world of science today as Hans' Law of Equine Motivation.

On the other hand, Hans found there were distinct advantages to putting the horse behind the cart. It was possible to build a shelf on the back of the cart from which the horse could get his oats and water as he ambled along, thus saving the time for feeding stops. For another thing, horses are notoriously careless in their personal habits and, with horses *behind* carts, they did not offend the drivers or violate good manners.

If only the Dutch had allowed Hans to perfect his invention, Holland might have saved untold millions of hours of man and horsepower in gathering cheeses and become an all-time Great Power.

Professor Carstairs had something of the same experience when he was a young graduate student. He was studying snowflakes. He was aware of the old belief that no two snowflakes are *ever* alike, but one day he found he could produce identical snowflakes in an ice cream mixer in the laboratory. He rushed to his professor with his microscope, crying: "Look, three snowflakes absolutely identical in every respect!"

The professor looked and said: "Carstairs, you're too big for this school. If word of this were to get out, they would burn us down. People have believed for too long that no two snowflakes are ever alike to accept this breakthrough. My advice to you is to give up science and go into psychology where there is plenty of room for exceptions."

* * *

I see where an animal psychologist predicts that eventually we will train monkeys and birds to do many of the distastefully routine jobs in Our Society, just as porpoises are now being trained. He says they will do farm work, weeding, picking fruit and work in factory assembly lines. That term, "animal psychologist," confuses me. I get a mental picture of an animal which has been trained in psychology, maybe a bear, or even a horse with a Ph.D. in the psychology of racing.

There are such horses, of course, I've bet on them many times without realizing they were in a race more to study the behavior of other horses than to finish as winners themselves. About winning they couldn't care less. They drop behind almost from the moment they leave the gate so they can observe the behavior of the whole field in front of them, right down to the wire. Sometimes they are equally interested in people, too and will pause in the homestretch to observe the behavior of the people in the stands who have put money down on them to win, place, or show, and who are now waving them on with rage.

Well, this man who is an animal psychologist has tried using pigeons in a pilot project that makes me wonder. He taught them to attend the conveyor line moving contraceptive pills to the bottling area. The pigeons would study the pills and tap a signal device, once for a good pill and twice for a defective one. The way I understand it, a number of plain aspirin pills were thrown in with the birth-control pills in a test, and the pigeons caught every one of the aspirins.

Now I ask you, if your family planning and budgeting is dependent on getting the right pill, would you care to leave that responsibility to a pigeon? If a pigeon hates people or goes to work some day not caring much about his job, there could be bright, new little faces in high chairs at dining room tables all over the country a year or so later.

I wouldn't care to have monkeys sorting the pill, either. Monkeys may be dedicated and it may be possible to induce them to work long hours on the production line, but monkeys are notorious for monkeying around. And sure as shooting, Ms. Foster in the stenographers' pool is going to have to take maternity leave that she hadn't planned.

There is some comfort in the fact that the president of the pharmaceutical company, where the experiment with the pigeons was made, announced he had stopped the program because he was afraid when the news got out he wouldn't be able to sell even a soda pill to anyone except members of the Audubon Society.

It is only a matter of time, the animal psychologist insists, until macaws and cockatoos and parrots will be answering telephones when you call a company with a complaint. Getting complaints ironed out will be even more dreadful an undertaking when you have to fight parrots saying "Pretty Polly" as well as recalcitrant computers.

The psychologist claims he has taught monkeys to pick fruit for a monetary reward – not much, just a few pennies – and that monkeys can understand money as a reward and be taught that it can be spent for goodies, bananas or other fruits. How long are monkeys going to be satisfied with a banana or two when they realize that four bananas are better? And begin to demand shorter hours and more pay? Inevitably, they will want job security and pensions and sick benefits and portal-to-portal pay and all the rest of it. The trouble with scientists is that they don't think these things through.

Years ago I wouldn't have understood why there would be any fuss about pigeons monitoring The Pill. I thought when talk about the Pill started everyone meant aspirin, and I couldn't understand all the excitement. Ladies would come up to me to make small talk at cocktail parties and would say: "What do you think about The Pill?" And I would say: "Oh, I don't know." And they would say: "Well what about the safety of The Pill?" And I would say: "I have been using the pill for years, for headaches or when I had the flu, and it has never occurred to me that safety was involved. Of course, any drug can become addictive if it is used psychologically as a crutch."

And then the ladies would say: "What are you, some kind of a big nut or something?" and I was puzzled. I remember one woman complained to the hostess. She had asked me if I thought married women should take The Pill and I said: "Well, surely, if a woman's husband takes the pill, and if she gives them to her children, I can't see any reason in the world why she shouldn't take the pill herself." And she stomped away and told the hostess that I had accused her of giving The Pill to her young daughters. Well, I didn't know she had daughters and I had no idea what kind of pill she was talking about. The world goes so fast these days you can't keep up with everything.

Green Eyes finally took me aside and explained to me that The Pill wasn't aspirin, but she never did succeed in making me understand how it works – it is the most absurd thing I ever heard and directly conflicts with everything I was told when I was a kid. I was told that the doctor brings babies in his little black bag, and it was a comfort to hear, and I still believe it no matter what anybody says. The only difference today is that now the doctor brings them to the hospital, not to your house.

I remember when Green Eyes and I were driving away from our wedding in a taxicab, I said: "Well, we are married and now we will call the doctor and have him bring us a baby in his little black bag," and the cab driver turned and said: "Lady, do you want me to take you back to the church? It may not be too late to get it undone."

CHAPTER VIII

Travel

So I said to Green Eyes: "What are you doing?" And she said: "Packing the medicine case for our vacation." And I said: "We're not going to need any medicine for the kind of vacation we're taking this year. We're roughing it, sleeping in a mountain meadow with a blanket, taking a quick dip in an alpine lake, frying fresh fish for breakfast."

And she said: "Oh, fine. That's why I'm packing medicine. These are eyedrops to get ashes out of your eyes." And I said: "How am I going to get ashes in my eyes?" And she said: "When you blow on the fire that's cooking the fish." And I said: "I don't blow on fires, I fan them. I was a Boy Scout. I can read Indian signs. Indians used to come to me to take lessons."

And she said: "I don't know what's got into you to take this kind of vacation. You won't be able to pick up a telephone and order room service." And I said: "Everybody's going back to getting in touch with nature and our primitive origins." And she said: "You haven't far to go."

And I said: "What's in that nasty-looking bottle?" And she said: "It's stuff for mosquitoes." And I said: "I forgot about mosquitoes. What is in that blue bottle?" And she said: "It's a little something to ease your stomach pains until we can get you down from the hills to a doctor for surgery." And I said: "How am I going to get stomach pain? We're going to eat simple, natural food in the Great Outdoors." And she said: "It neutralizes the sand and twigs and bugs that fall into the scrambled eggs and the beef jerky you wolf down."

And I said: "Oh, that's silly. All we really need is an earache remedy for icy winds when we get up to snowline, and headache pills for when I don't have my martini before dinner and maybe a tranquilizer if I see a bear." And she said: "And these few bandages and an antibiotic for when you cut yourself." And I said: "When do I cut myself?" And she said: "When you cut kindling for the fire. Do you think you could type with only one arm?"

And I said: "I tell you what. Let's alter our plans a little. Let's go to a first-class resort in the mountains, one with room service. But bring along your medicines in case it's the house physician's night off."

We never go on a trip anywhere without Green Eyes' pills. She's been saving pills for years and we have a walk-in medicine cabinet with pills stacked from floor to ceiling, all indexed. The local hospitals like to know there is always a supply of every kind of pill at our house when a certain one is not available through suppliers. The other day a gentleman was plucking feebly at his coverlet in a hospital with only seconds to spare and the doctors were arranging to jet a special pill in from New York when someone thought of Green Eyes. When I answered the phone they asked me if she had that pill and I said certainly, everyone knows she has every kind of pill. Green Eyes wasn't home but I finally found the pill in her brown handbag and sent it down to the hospital and the patient was up and demanding a pepperoni pizza by evening.

* * *

It's been years since we took a long vacation by automobile. It used to be pleasant. You'd drive along and there would be a sign: "Historical Marker," and your wife would cry out: "Oh, Historical Marker!" And you would say: "Where?"

And she would say: "About a quarter of a mile back, now." And you'd back up and two or three other cars would go in the ditch and the Historical Marker would say: "Fried Mush Creek. Here, in the summer of 1849, Captain Solomon Ribbentrop camped and fried some mush for breakfast while surveying the Pacific Railroad."

And then your wife would say: "It's like living with history, isn't it?"

Today you whiz by on a freeway and all you see is a sign on an offramp telling you that somewhere way off on a side road is the marker for Fried Mush Creek. All the romance is gone.

Also, there was a time when you could ask a motel operator or gas station attendant where State 27 intersected with US 60. He would say: "You go down the road eleven miles until you come to Joe Mooney's place under the weeping willows and then you turn right at the big mossy rock. But mind you, there's a mud hole about three hundred feet from the turn and you'll find Joe there with his horse. He'll pull you out of the hole for ten dollars. When he isn't pulling out autos he uses the horse to haul water to the hole."

Today nobody knows anything. Nobody has been working at the gas station longer than a week. "Gee, I don't know much about this part of the country. I've been here only a short time myself." You say: "How far is it to Bent Elbow?" And he says: "I may be able to tell you if you tell me one thing first. What state is this?"

* * *

We have stayed at this deluxe mountain resort in Northern California, and it is so far back in the hills that the room-service waiters are bears. It is a little shocking to order an intimate dinner for two and have a bear appear and flame your shishkabob. A bear brought our breakfast in the morning too. He was not too tidy but he was breaking in and doing his best.

He was moody. He said a man from the union was up to organize the place and was startled to find some of the employees were bears. There is no provision in the union charter for bears and there is no possible way, our bear said, for them to write in a "hibernation clause."

We asked our bear waiter where the action was around the joint and he said some of the guests like to sit outside on the covered porch and watch it rain, and some walk up the back trail a few hundred yards to see the chipmunks. There were some new chipmunks in from Tahoe – a great act – although they work for peanuts. There was also a poker game in our wing which started in 1958 and hadn't stopped since.

Some guests visit the garbage dump to watch the room-service bears eat. Our bear said bitterly that he and other bear employees were paid off in table scraps. The other bears didn't care much but he was not content with being a bear. He wanted to be people. He was real sore at the resort management. Our bear had to wait until Friday night to collect his week's tips that had been written on the tabs by the guests, and he couldn't wait to start his own place.

I once stayed at a Viking-type ski lodge on Whitefish Lake at Big Mountain, Montana, and the room-service waiter there turned out to be a bear, too. Everything around there was Norwegian in decor, but you really haven't lived until you see a room-service waiter who is a bear wearing a bronze Viking helmet with horns.

And I said: "Good heavens, aren't you the same bear who was the room-service waiter at Wilderness Enow in California a few years back? What are you doing here?"

And he said: "They finally organized that joint and they wouldn't let no bears into the union."

And I said: "I didn't know you worked winters anywhere. I thought all bears were hibernating this time of year."

And he said: "Look, Doc, I don't tell you how to run your business, so why don't you leave me run mine?"

He didn't have much to say except that tips were smaller here than in California. He also said that between shifts he sometimes goes up Big Mountain to ski.

And I said: "You mean you ski with people?"

And he said, frowning: "Is there anything wrong with that? You think bears aren't good enough to ski with people? Are you a bigot?"

So the next day I was with some ski-types in the bar at Big Mountain Chalet and I heard one ski-type say to another ski-type: "I saw a bear skiing on Mully's Mile today." And the second ski-type thought about it for a while and finally said: "I believe that is a reasonable statement." And the first ski-type said: "And I want to tell you, when I passed him he was filling up a sitzmark. He had just crashed and burned." And the second ski-type said: "I believe that is a reasonable statement too."

And I turned to these two ski-types and said: "I couldn't help overhearing what you said about a bear skiing. I think I know that bear, he is a room-service waiter down at the lake. Was he wearing a bronze Viking helmet?"

Both ski-types were silent for a time and finally one said to me: "I salute you. I believe you have been longer in this bar than either of us." Which wasn't true at all, I'd just got there.

I was afraid my bear friend might wander into one of the traps that the Forest Service people had set out to catch bears for removal to another watershed. One night a fellow was baiting one of the traps with fresh fish. The trap is a short section of steel culvert with bars at one end and a barred door at the other. A black bear came up while the fellow's back was turned, and, when the fellow saw the bear, he slammed the door in panic and locked himself in the trap. He swears that the bear let him out, stepped politely aside while he came out, and then went in and ate the fish.

It couldn't have been my bear friend because he wouldn't eat raw fish, I'm sure. He nibbled on the orders he brought from the kitchen to the rooms – cooked stuff. It was one way of making up for the short tips he got around there.

* * *

Remember when travelers used to carry money with them instead of credit cards? Hotel and motel operators can't recall that far back. In our resort hotel room we found a card on the door: "If you plan to pay your account by check, please call the manager's office before noon to make arrangements. Thank you for your cooperation." They didn't fool me. They weren't thanking me, they were just as good as accusing me of fixing to pay my way out with a bum check.

I said to Green Eyes: "I wonder what kind of an arrangement could be made to pay cash." And she said: "Please, we were going to have a nice quiet vacation. No gags." But I called the manager anyway and said: "What kind of arrangement can I make to pay my way out of here with cash?" And he said: "You mean *cash* – tens and twenties and that sort of thing?" And I said: "Yes, cash money." And he said: "Perhaps you have some credit card which we could stretch a point to recognize and send your bill later to your office."

And we said firmly: "No, cash." And he said: "We are not set up for cash." And we said: "Well, get set up." And he said: "It would confuse our cashier to have real money. She doesn't know how to handle it." And I said: "I insist on my right to pay my obligations in the legal currency of the realm." And he said: "Look, let me issue you one of our credit cards. I won't ask you a single question and I will send up a couple rounds of drinks and hors d'oeuvres, compliments of the house." And I said: "Okay."

That night he phoned and told me apologetically that he had a convention coming in next noon and the house was completely booked, including our room. And when I told Green Eyes we had to pack and move on she glared at me and said: "Oh, great! Big funny man with gags!"

* * *

The cash flow is pretty steady when you travel with a woman, even if you do use credit cards. Women are always asking for money to tip in powder rooms, and the going rate for tips keeps climbing. The tip used to be a quarter, although I once had a lady ask me to give her a dollar for a powder room tip and I never got back the change. It was at Club 21 in New York, and Green Eyes and I had been invited for dinner there by some nice people who print their own money, and when the hostess wanted to retire to the powder room her husband was visiting at another table and she said to me: "Lover, may I have a dollar?" So I gave her a dollar although I had to reach in and unpin it from my underwear.

When she came back I wanted to ask her about what kind of a place it was because I figured I had a vested interest in it. I was wondering especially how much a lady attendant could knock off in a single night at a dollar a throw.

Green Eyes went three times to the powder room and started to go the fourth time and I whispered: "Aren't you running up a pretty good bill? You are already into me for three dollars." And she said: "I don't leave a dollar. I leave fifty cents." And I said: "You are making us look like peasants. Word has probably reached the maitre d' that you leave only fifty cents." And she said: "It's not worth a dollar." And I said: "Then stay out of the place."

Well, I went to the boy's room at Club 21 and there was an attendant there who handed out towels and combs and hair blowers and beside him was a dish of quarters and half-dollars and, obviously, the going rate there was considerably less than in the powder room. But having given my hostess and Green Eyes dollars to maintain their status in the powder room, I couldn't do less for myself, and I laid a dollar bill in the dish and the attendant said: "God bless you, sir!" and he whiskbroomed me all the way back to my table.

* * *

My neighbors the Blairs and their kids are just back from their vacation, and it's going to be an uphill job for Mrs. Blair to get Mr. Blair to go holidaying with her again.

When Blair goes on a vacation he likes to go to some distant resort four days drive away, and he gets behind the wheel and puts about eight hundred miles behind him every day. Mrs. Blair says to her children at breakfast on these trips: "Don't drink milk or anything this morning because you know Daddy won't stop." And at the end of the day it takes two men to lift Mr. Blair out of his car and straighten him up, and sometimes he carries the steering wheel right into the motel with him.

Mrs. Blair was determined that this year's trip would be different. About last January she started a campaign to spend this year's vacation at a farm – not a dude ranch – just a peaceful farm not too far away, where the children could get back to nature. She said instead of Mr. Blair killing himself driving he could sit on the front porch with her and rock all day, watching the children romp through the fields and play with the animals.

There was a loud scream at this from their oldest girl who only wants to go where there are boys, but Mrs. Blair paid no attention, saying the girl should think of her father's health. He could help the farmer with the work, and the exercise would be good for him. Then Mr. Blair screamed, stating flatly that he wasn't going to help any farmer do his work and pay $300 a week for the privilege. But Mrs. Blair wheedled and importuned him and used her feminine wiles, and he finally said yes.

The farm was only a hundred miles away and they arrived before breakfast, and they found the farmer's wife cooking doughnuts in a bucket full of hot fat. She had already cooked about four dozen doughnuts, and Mrs. Blair said in astonishment: "Who are all these for?" And the lady farmer said: "These are just a little snack to go with your ham and eggs and sausages for breakfast instead of hotcakes." And Mrs. Blair said: "Oh, Mr. Blair and I eat very light breakfasts, just fruit and coffee." And Mr. Blair said: "Today we will eat doughnuts. We'll probably put on twenty pounds a week, but this was your idea. On a farm you eat like a farmer."

The accommodations were all right, two little rooms and a private bath on the second floor, except that the bath wasn't working. An antique facility in the back yard beyond the chicken coop had been pressed into temporary service.

Lunch was two kinds of meat, five vegetables, fresh bread and two kinds of pie, all delicious, and Mrs. Blair was torn between tasting everything and preserving her slimming diet, which was a real battle. But Mr. Blair ate heartily and shamed Mrs. Blair by unzipping the top of his pants to make room.

The small children went exploring ecstatically through the fields, and it took two hours to pull the ticks off them when they returned. The oldest girl said she was going to walk to the nearest town and take the next bus back home *right that minute* it was so *boring,* but about then the farmer's college son drove up. He wasn't exactly the handsomest boy in the world but he was older than the Blair girl and he was a *boy.* He wasn't too articulate, either, but he managed an offer to take her to a dance that night, and she brightened perceptibly.

Blair might have adjusted to rural life except that the lady farmer belonged to a church that frowned on booze, so Blair had to have his evening cocktail in his room. "Why can't you forget the cocktail and just sit on the porch with me and drink in the beauty and peace of this pastoral scene?" Mrs. Blair asked. And Mr. Blair said: "You run your life and I'll run mine."

It didn't work out too well. What with cocktails in his room and eating so much he could scarcely move out of his dining room chair, Mr. Blair didn't get to breathe much of that good, clean outdoors air and never did get exercise out in the alfalfa field, and Mrs. Blair found her pants were unaccountably shrinking. But the Blair's oldest girl had a wonderful time and a couple of nights she didn't come home until 3:00 A.M. The other children got bitten and developed nettle rashes, and one came home with an arm in a sling.

Mrs. Blair said it would have been a wonderful vacation if Mr. Blair had adapted to farm life. The oldest Blair girl adapted best; she's still writing to the farmer's son and trying to promote an exchange vacation next summer at the Blair home.

* * *

So Green Eyes and I came to this southern resort for rest and a little sun and to get away from our neighbors. Now all of a sudden, who is in the next lanai to ours? The McMurty's, our next door neighbors at home! And they tell me that Dorothy Leighton, the neighbor I can't stand, and her husband are due tomorrow.

It's my fault. I opened my big mouth at the Coopers' a week ago and told everybody about the wonderful resort place I'd found with kitchens and private lanais, and a big swimming pool, and orange and lemon trees growing outside your front door and lizards a foot long looking in your windows begging for table scraps.

I came out of my door one morning and here was Mrs. McMurty by the pool in a swimsuit. Like I keep telling you, she is 40-40-40 straight up and down, and in a swimsuit she looks like an inflated life raft. I mean, when she jumps in the pool the water rises right over the rim.

After breakfast she came over and said to Green Eyes: "Why don't you make him go out and sit in the sun?" And I said: "I will go out and sit in the sun when I am darned good and ready to go out and sit in the sun." And she said: "Stay here if you like, but I am going to ask your good wife to help me with my hair and I expect to help her blow-dry her hair." And I said: "I am now darn good and ready to sit in the sun." If there is anyplace no man should be, it is where two women start fooling around with their hair.

I went next door to see McMurty. It was nine in the morning and already he had a frosted drink in his hand. He goes to resorts to drink cool refreshments and play gin rummy, and he never goes outdoors. He feels the outdoors is greatly overrated.

"Take any card," he said, "it's your turn to deal. Put on a green eyeshade and pull up a chair and some money." And I said: "How can you get smashed so soon after breakfast?" And he said: "It's easy. Tequila martinis, ten parts tequila, one part vermouth, two drops lemon juice and a blaster." And I said: "What's a blaster?" And he said: "A pickled hot pepper."

And I said: "I got half a mind to go tell your wife you're sailing." And he said: "She knows it. We have a deal. On vacations she lets me drink as long as I don't say anything about how she looks in a swimsuit." Like all ideal marriages, the McMurtys' is based on a community of interests. They share the same dislikes – each other.

So I had a tequila martini, and I can't rightly decide whether it tastes like kerosene or paint thinner. All I can say is after you swallow the tequila, that pickled pepper tastes like sugar candy.

Dorothy Leighton and her husband arrived that afternoon and took the unit on the other side of us, and she immediately began to organize. She can't just sit in a chair and bake, she's got to have people working for her. She called a conference and proposed pooling the commissary and cooking everything in *my* kitchen because it's the largest. She appointed Mrs. McMurty the breakfast chef, Green Eyes dinner chef, and she would be lunch chef and maitre d', or boss.

I believe in being polite to ladies even when I hate them, so I said to Dorothy Leighton: "Nothing doing. I'm not going to have you running in and out of my place. I came on this trip only to get away from people like you." And she said, equally gently: "Nobody cares what you think about anything."

So they took a vote and I lost and now my place is full of women and I can't walk around in my shorts any more, Green Eyes won't let me. You should have seen what Mrs. McMurty cooked for breakfast next morning, hot cakes and Spanish omelet and pounds of bacon and pig sausages and there went my diet!

At lunch they wanted to picnic. I stayed home to write but I told them a place to go. They left with forty-eight sandwiches, and later Green Eyes asked where I told them to picnic. And I said: "At the end of the road on Rattlesnake Hill." And she said: "Why, good heavens, at this time of year it is simply crawling with snakes and poisonous spiders and gila monsters!" And I said: "I know, I know." But they came back later and had only some deep cactus wounds and half a dozen black-widow-spider bites.

Dorothy Leighton was the biggest problem. She ran into our place every other minute with a Project. She wanted something moved or somebody to drive her to town. She wasn't content to wear out her own husband, she had to work on the rest of us, too. She came to me with a Big Idea. The local newspaper had a story that volunteers were wanted to lick envelopes for mailing for a charity event. She wanted me to get out of my poolside chair and lick envelopes.

I said: "Have you any idea what licking envelopes all afternoon would do to the sensitive taste buds in my tongue? I wouldn't be able to taste McMurty's tequila martinis tonight." And she said: "There is no community spirit in you at all. You don't care about little children." And I said: "I do care and I will give you some money to take to the committee, but I will not lick envelopes and endanger my taster and lose my standing as a professional martini drinker."

So she made her husband go and he came back with his tongue hanging down to the second button on his shirt. Even with two hands he couldn't get it back in.

She didn't ask McMurty to go. He just sat and never moved except to have another tequila martini or deal cards. And when they brought him something to eat he waited until no one was looking and tossed it over the wall. The scavenger birds circled overhead and watched him, and they had our meal hours down to the minute.

I do believe Dorothy Leighton did Great Good there. After only three days at the resort she was on two committees for the community charity circus, and when she read in the paper that the local Chamber of Commerce invited every resident to tell what should be done to make the town a finer and better place, she presented it with a complete agenda.

Meanwhile, Green Eyes and Mrs. McMurty were busy all day doing the housework and cooking.

I tell you this to show you how well three couples can get along together on a vacation.

I discussed this vacation business with two neighbors who are authorities on human behavior, Dr. Spook, our psychiatrist, and Professor Carstairs, our psychologist, who was the first man ever to run a cat through a puzzle-box and was, later, the first man, again, to run a puzzle-box through a cat, which is a good deal harder to do because you end up with a square cat.

Dr. Spook said that people have turned their own homes into vacation substitutes in recent years, living informally and casually, and the need for vacations is not as great as it used to be. He said also that the average home cook today turns out better food than the average resort hotel. Well, I don't know about that. I've never had a resort hotel serve me a TV dinner on a divided foil plate. Why, some of the cooks around here don't even pull the top off before they shove it in the oven.

All I could get Professor Carstairs to say was that all he asked of a vacation was to be able to get away from Mrs. Carstairs, and he would enjoy it just as much if she went to live on the other side of town.

* * *

I was on this Amtrak daycoach and the kid across the aisle was in a space-suit and was trying to make train noises. He said "whoosh" and "pit, pit, pit" and "kuh kuh."

And I said to Green Eyes: "There is the modern generation for you. The little beggar can't even make a proper train noise. Do you think his mother would mind if I told him how to make train noises?"

And she said: "Leave well enough alone. He's making enough noise already."

And I said: "But trains do not make a kuh-kuh noise and somebody ought to set the little beggar straight. It's probably his first train ride and he'll go through life thinking that trains go kuh-kuh.

And she said: "How do trains go?"

And I said: "Everybody knows how trains go. They go

choo-choo and they whistle whah-whah-wa-whah. That third wa is important. It's different."

And she said: "Do diesel electric locomotives go choo-choo?"

And I said: "For a woman and a wife you know entirely too much. For heaven sake, there is such a thing as poetic license, you know. Nobody has ever been able to imitate the sound of one of these nasty diesels, so there is kind of an understanding among us older kids that diesels still go choo-choo."

And she said: "You're asking for trouble. In another minute he'll be over in your lap – and he's eating a warm chocolate bar."

So I said to the kid: "How does a train go?"

And the kid looked at me distrustfully a moment and then described an arc with his hand and said: "Plop!"

And I said incredulously: "A train goes plop?"

And he said: "A cannon."

And I said: "A cannon goes whissssssh and then *boom!*"

And he said: "Plop."

And I said to Green Eyes: "Gee, the kid doesn't even know how a cannon goes. Even as stupid a kid as I was, I knew it goes whisssh and boom."

And the kid said "Plop" again. I said: "Is this your first ride on a choo-choo, son?"

And his mother said: "He's been on a train before."

And I said to her: "Hasn't he learned that a train goes choo-choo and the whistle goes whah-whah-wa-whah?"

The kid made a horrible noise of a jet taking off.

His mama said: "He hasn't met an authority on train noises until now."

The kid said: "Ding-ding-ding."

And I said: "Ding-ding-ding is not a train noise. It's a streetcar. Where did he ever hear a streetcar in these days?"

And the mother said: "It's not a streetcar. It is a San Francisco *cable* car."

And Green Eyes said: "Some big expert you are! You don't

know a streetcar noise from a cable car – and at your age!"

And I said: "I know a San Francisco cable-car noise. It is not ding-ding-ding. It is like a drum beat. It is ding-ding-ding-*al-ling*!"

And the kid said: "Plop."

And I pointed my finger at him like a revolver and said: "Bang!"

And he pointed his finger at me and said: "Khaaaah!"

And I said: "He doesn't even know how to fire a gun. Guns go *Bang*. They don't go Khaaaah."

We were in the last car and the flagman was sitting there ahead of us and now he got into it.

"A diesel," he says, "growls. It goes grrrrrrrrrr."

I suppose because the flagman is wearing a uniform and I'm not, the kid listens. He goes 'grrrrrrrrrr." And the flagman says: "Now you got it."

And the kid described another arc with his hand and said "Plop" and destroyed us all.

CHAPTER IX

Birds and Beasts

The Audubon Society surely has given me up for good by this time. I can't say I blame them. I forgot again this year to count birds for the Society's annual census. When I forgot last year they sent me a gently reproving letter: "Look, Welch, either you count birds or you don't count birds. There can be no compromise." They were nice about it, but firm.

The target date this year was New Year's Day. I had my binoculars and pencil and paper and bird-counting suit all laid out for the occasion, but when New Year's day came around I was not feeling well. There was a lot of malaise, in fact, all around our neighborhood that day, and we must have caught it from someone. Bright and early however, like, oh say 11:30 A.M., I was up and off to count birds. "I am going to count birds," I said to Green Eyes gaily, and she said, rather coldly: "It figures." She disapproves of the temperance group I belong to and whose meeting I had attended the night before. She does not subscribe to our belief that the way to get liquor off the market is to exhaust the supply.

The only other fellow counting birds was Mr. Dibble, who lives in the next block and who swims out in our lake for sticks his dog throws into the water for him to retrieve. Of course, sometimes his wife throws sticks for him, too. For Christmas his family gave him one of those whistles that are pitched so high you can scarcely hear them, but strangely enough, he can hear it loud and clear.

"Does your dog come when you blow the whistle?" I asked him, and he said: "You got it wrong. The dog blows the whistle and I come." Two or three times while we were counting birds the dog blew the whistle for him but he wouldn't go. "I've got rights," he kept saying. "He knows I'm busy."

First he would count a bird and then I would count a bird. Once he accused me of counting his bird a second time, but he didn't come right out and say I was cheating. My list was longer than his because I applied a wife-and-husband factor to each bird I counted. I multiplied by two on the theory that each bird had someone pretty special waiting for him or her at home.

It was bitterly cold, but fortunately, I had provided some tea and gave him some. "This is great tea," he said, "what kind is it?" And I said: "It's Kentucky tea." So then his dog came to see why he wasn't answering the whistle and took Mr. Dibble home. And I went home, too, with only twenty-six birds accounted for. It isn't much of a report, but it's the best I could do under the circumstances. Green Eyes was no help, either. "Only twenty-six," she said. "I imagine they were all vultures and were circling around above you."

While we were counting the birds, Mr. Dibble told me that he also has a bird whistle guaranteed to call anything from a bluejay to an American bald eagle. He saw an ad for it in a magazine before Christmas and told Mrs. Dibble that he would like one of those, too, in his stocking Christmas morning. And she said: "For heaven's sake, why do you want to call birds?" And he said: "Because I believe it would give me quite a sense of mastery to be able to step out of my house and call our little feathered friends to my side." And she said: "You've been at the cooking sherry again."

But he found the whistle in his stocking Chistmas morning, with a book saying the best time to call birds is at dawn. Birds are not like people. Birds get up early in the

McCAUSLAND

morning feeling fine and alert. So the day after Christmas Dibble was out with his whistle calling birds like mad at 5:30 A.M. I slipped pants over my pajamas and went up the street to warn him to run for the hills before the neighbors organized a vigilante group and burned down his house.

About the time I reached him, his wife came out and shouted she was going to leave him, but it struck me it would be no great loss – the way Mrs. Dibble does her hair up for the night and creams her face, she looks worse than Humpty Dumpty after his fall.

Dibble said he was going to throw away the whistle anyway because all it attracted was robins. Apparently, the whistle made them furious and they were dive-bombing him. What Dibble was telling them with his whistle obviously was frightfully insulting and perhaps even obscene.

I was painting my fence yesterday and thinking about birds, and I looked up and, sure enough, circling above my head in the sky were half a dozen birds just waiting to alight on the fence as soon as I went into the house. I try to be charitable about birds sitting on my fence. I understand they have to sit somewhere. I am not sure why they prefer my fence to trees. I keep changing the color of it to fool them, to find a color that will suit us both, but sooner or later comes some bird with different decorating ideas than mine.

I have a wild cherry tree in my yard that produces berries so bitter that if you eat one your lips will pucker permanently as well as your stomach. I suppose the birds find these cherries equally bitter, but they flock madly to my tree when it is heavy with fruit, and then they perch on my fence. Frankly, I have never considered this a proper way for the birds to show their appreciation of my thoughtfulness in insuring their regularity.

A fellow in the Foresty Service says that cities are full of unexpected places for wild animals to live. He says he's found squirrels and raccoons and skunks and wood rats and exotic birds living in cities, and he thinks this is a good thing. He says city-dwellers must be cured of the "neatness syndrome" and have a program of "planned neglect" in order to induce wild animals to live among us.

Now I happen to know that a couple of raccoons live in the Bazettis' yard down the street in my neighborhood. I think what attracts them there is (1) the Bazettis always leave their garage door open in the front of their house and you can look in and see the old toidy chair smack in the middle of the garage along with accumulated junk. (2) The Bazettis almost never cut their back lawn because Mr. Bazetti orders his oldest boy to do it and the kid doesn't want to. (3) There is an old bathtub with claw feet in the backyard which Mr. Bazetti plans to convert into a planter some day. Here, surely, is "planned neglect," and their yard is an ideal place for wild life to gather and a wonderful place, too, for kids to get wet and run screaming home when they fall into the rain and sprinkler water that gathers in the bathtub.

I have seen the raccoons in the Bazetti yard. They live under the poison-ivy vines, which are another great attraction of the place, and they even come out and feed from the hand when we sit around on the patio at one of Bazetti's wine-tasting parties. He regularly puts down enough wine each year to float the Queen Elizabeth, which is why he can't get around to weeding the flower beds. Still, they are nice people and very friendly and kind, and if you live near them, all you need is a high fence to shut the untidiness out.

We have rats in the neighborhood, too, although I am not sure they are wood rats. They exist on the Fullers' uncovered compost pits, which are about the size of a small town's sewage settling-basin system. In the heat of summer we sometimes gather in one another's yard and there is rough, belligerent talk about it, but the Fullers insist they are not attracting rats with their compost pit. They say the rats are attracted by Hixly, who puts ground-up fish heads on his lawn. On a hot day his place smells like a three-dollar shore dinner. This also attracts cats and I suppose they are "wild life," too.

I have a number of birds on my place because I put out grain soaked in whiskey, and the word has gone around among the feathered dipsomaniacs. I have a telescope on my desk and a tree outside the window where the birds gather, and I am trying to determine whether birds have more than one facial expression. So far they are pretty much like John Wayne, two expressions – hat on and hat off. You can't tell when they are happy or sad. But you can sure tell when they are loaded.

There is also a barn owl who stays in our second-story porch. I suggested once to Green Eyes that she go to the Bazettis and get some mice for him. I am sure the Bazettis have mice to spare, but she wouldn't go. Instead, she fixed the owl up with about two bucks of raw ground beef and he ate it and has been eating it ever since.

I have never seen him eating any of the whiskey-soaked grain, and once I fixed him a dish of oats into which I had spooned some martini, very dry. He never touched it. He may be wiser than I think.

* * *

The government is always doing some kind of a study on wild animals, and some of the studies turn out to be downright embarrassing for the creatures. Take that study the government did a few years back in Alaska on the migration patterns of bears. They painted the hindquarters of bears so they could be easily followed.

They had two ways to paint the bears. One was to wait on the trail until a bear came along minding his own business, and the government man, as the bear passed, shot him with a plastic bullet containing green dye, and – wham, whoosh – all of a sudden the bear was wearing green shorts he couldn't take off. This set him apart from fellow bears. They would examine him in astonishment and say things like: "Well, I see you are all dressed for the party," and "I've heard of painting the town red, but this is ridiculous!" and like that.

And the painted bear would say: "There's some joker up on the hill. But I rather like it. It fits snug, but I guess they didn't have my size. I didn't know I had it until I reached for my wallet. . . ."

The other way to paint a bear was to creep into a cave during the winter when he was hibernating. The government man had more leisure in this instance and could paint figures or designs or what pleased his fancy. And when the bear woke up in the spring, his wife would say: "Well, I see you are licensed to carry 4,000 pounds." And the bear would back up to the mirror and scream: "I wish you'd watch the kids when I'm sleeping."

And she'd walk down the trail behind him, laughing fit to kill, and – wham – a government man would let her have it, perhaps in yellow, and they'd show up at a bear rendezvous, he wearing license plates and she in a colored bikini.

The government men who painted the hibernating bears while they were asleep in the caves also took their temperatures to determine their body heat and spoke to the bears to see how deeply they slept. I mean they would say, "How are you, madam?" and "Where's the action around here?" and like that.

There was only one untoward incident where a lady bear mumbled in her sleep and folded her great arms around the government man and snuggled for two or three days. He finally got away, the story goes, by saying: "I'll be right back." The government man's wife was furious about his absence and not in the least appeased by his incredible story.

"What kind of bear was this?" she asked, "a lady bear or a male bear?" And he said: "It was a lady bear and, actually, she was rather nice."

The government men were heroes, of course, when they returned from Alaska, and were often asked at parties exactly what they did in Alaska. And they would say: "We crawled into caves and stuck thermometers into bears." And people would say: "Well, there you go – silly question, silly answer."

* * *

Everyone who lives in a typically American neighborhood like mine seems to think a pet of some kind is a requirement. We have plenty of dogs and cats and now we have *chickens!* The owner is nutty Mrs. Peterson, the same Mrs. Peterson who thumbs her nose at Fred, the mailman, when he hasn't any mail to leave her, and Fred gets terribly hurt because, basically, he wants people to love him.

We used to wonder about our property values dropping when Mrs. Peterson thumbed her nose at Fred, but now that she has chickens we don't wonder any more. We *know* they are dropping. There isn't a house in the block that hasn't dropped in value since Mrs. Peterson got herself twenty hens and one rooster. It is against the law to keep chickens here in quantity, but nobody wants to be the first to put the finger on her. She claims they are pets.

This rooster – I can't wait until he is a chicken-in-a-pot – he thinks he is a cuckoo. He crows on the hour and half hour and any time a truck passes. He even gets up at 2 A.M. to crow when Carter next door comes home late and his headlights shine in the chicken yard. The rooster crows and then all the dogs take up the alarm and we are all taking sleeping pills like salted peanuts.

I mean, we keep our houses painted and our lawns mowed, and grub in our flower beds to have one of the prettiest neighborhoods in the state, and all of a sudden we got cockle-doodle-doo and kut-kut-kadawkut. The hens are sore about something and squawk all day long. The rooster crows and then the hens tell him off. But, of course, how can you expect twenty hens to be happy with only one top man?

Heaven knows we have all tried to be nice to Mrs.

Peterson. I have even tried to talk her out of her notion that The President reads her mail. It was that time that she told me that chickens raised on an assembly-line chicken farm – "factory birds" she called them – don't taste as good as the old chicken-yard chickens who had to scratch for a living. She said factory birds today taste like the fishmeal they are fed, and heaven help me, I agreed with her because I wanted to get her off the subject of The President reading her mail.

So now she goes around telling everyone that I agreed chickens would taste better if she raised them herself and people are blaming me for her chicken yard. They are calling me "chicken-lover," and even The Widow stopped her car beside me the other day and said: "Well, now that you have encouraged Mrs. Peterson to keep chickens and make a shambles of a nice neighborhood, what do you propose to get rid of them?"

I hear that McMurty has offered a dollar each for a live chicken to any adventurous boy in the neighborhood. Carter threw a string of lighted firecrackers into the chicken pen last Thursday night when he came home from the annual banquet of the Sons of the Frozen North, but all that happened was the rooster crowed all night long and the hens never went to bed. Fuller is trying to buy a weasel or a raccoon to put in the chicken yard, and Dr. Spook is throwing in cracked corn soaked in feminine hormones. Already the rooster crows with a slight lisp.

I have spent a good deal of time among chickens during my disordered life, and, although I don't know enough chicken talk to speak it fluently, I do understand pretty well what is going on in a chicken yard. I have this big chicken suit I put on, and I sit on an apple box in some farmer's poultry yard and listen. I had a rooster suit at first, but I found it worried the hens almost out of their minds. Then I changed to a big hen suit and I seemed to equally worry roosters.

The first day I wore my hen suit I heard two roosters talking, one obviously the Head Man, and the other his executive officer. After looking me over from a distance, the Head Man said to his executive officer: "Well, I am taking the rest of the afternoon off and I am turning the whole command over to you." And the executive-officer-type rooster just stared at me and mumbled: "Gee, who's that big hen over there?" and the Head-Man rooster said: "It's up to you to go over and see." And the executive-officer-type rooster said: "Man, I ain't an executive-officer rooster, I'm just a capon."

I have found, after much time listening to hens, that they are full of criticism, fault-finding and rebellion against being subservient to roosters. I have never heard a single hen say anything nice about a rooster. The Head Man will get the hens lined up in the morning for roll call and he will crow a little and then say: "All right now, you hens, there are going to be a few changes in the pecking order around here. Desdemona, effective immediately, is Chief-Mistress Hen."

And the other hens cluck to one another: "Oh, her!" and "Well, I saw it coming," and "What he sees in her I can't imagine," and like that. But even when the Head Man is not changing the pecking order and is just policing the grounds and disciplining, the hens mutter: "Big deal," and "Who does he think he is?" and "What a loudmouth."

I must admit that I count the hours I have spent in the chicken suit in chicken yards as mostly wasted. In spite of my fluency in chicken language I still have trouble ordering egg foo yung on the dinner for three in Chinese restaurants.

You can't exactly call them pets, but Mr. Peabody is collecting fireflys. He says he thinks he has the energy shortage licked if he can gather enough of them and keep them functioning. He is pretty deep in studies of them and tells me that it is interesting stuff. He says that in some species both the male and female flash romantic invitations to one another; they apparently have no control over it, there is no switch to turn off their libidos.

Let's say a boy firefly is out for the evening and he's weary, weary, but he goes on flashing at intervals anyway like an illuminated sign. Presently a girl firefly shows up flashing, too, and she says: "Were you calling me, there, Percy?" And he says: "Not if I can help it, I wasn't. I don't have no control over my flashes, so bug off, will you?" And she says: "You're not so special, you know. This is the thirty-third false alarm I've logged tonight."

Mr. Peabody hopes to interbreed the fireflys with the strongest flashes and feed them vitamins and lots of protein and such, and eventually he expects to come up with a firefly which will flash at least five watts per bug. He is already working on a clear globe that will hold enough fireflys, with ample room to fly, to serve as illumination for an average room.

I think Mr. Peabody must have got his idea from my old friend, Professor Preston Carstairs, the behaviorist psychologist and tea-leaf reader, who has done research on the South American railroad bug which flashes two colors, red and green, and looks like a railroad train with running lights, even windows. Two or three of them flying nose-to-tail can give you quite a start. They flash at irregular intervals which leads some scientists to believe they are forming sentences.

Professor Carstairs says he has mastered the code and interpreted the message of one flashing railroad bug for whom other bugs seemed to be waiting in sidings. He says the first railroad bug was flashing to the waiting ones: "I am running twenty minutes late and have rights over all westbound bugs . . ." He had a dandy description of the sex life of the railroad bug in the paper he prepared for the next meeting of his fellow scientists. He claims even a casual date between two railroad bugs produces enough light to read a newspaper by.

Mr. Peabody argues that if the government can use porpoises in CIA work, he sees no reason why he can't interest high officials in the energy potential of fireflys.

Not all the pets in our neighborhood are fauna. Some are flora. Mrs. McMurty, for instance, has a collection of carnivorous, insectivorous and plain trap plants as pets. She read a paper about them at the Garden Club meeting at my house one day, and I got interested in them by listening to her paper from the top of the stairs, which I always do when the club meets at my house. You learn an awful lot about women when they aren't aware a man is listening, and I find that knowledge invaluable in writing and in dealing with Green Eyes – or, more truthfully, in her dealings with me.

Mrs. McMurty is crazy about creature-eating plants, and what she would really love to have is a carnivorous plant about the size of an apple tree which would lean over and devour Mr. McMurty some day when he is standing on his side of the rose bushes talking to The Widow in her yard.

Mrs. McMurty has a number of trap plants in a little hothouse in her back yard, and she feeds them chopped liver and flies and bees and raw meat, and you can hear them whining with hunger at feeding time each night. She has a Venus's-flytrap which she calls "Mama's Boy," and it lets her pet him, but it will close on anyone else's finger like a castanet.

Years ago, I remember, I went into Mrs. McMurty's hothouse to ask her something and I was eating a bologna sandwich. I recall that every plant in the place turned in my direction and stared meaningfully. If Mrs. McMurty would mow lawns like the other decent wives do, she wouldn't be 40-40-40 straight up and down and wouldn't have to submerge her consequent hostility into raising carnivorous plants, and I had gone in to her hothouse to tell her that. But one of her drosera growled at me and started to nibble my elbow, so I never did get to advise her.

I told Mr. McMurty how enthusiastically his wife read her paper about trap plants to the Garden Club and he said he thought it a good way to keep her attention off him. "She enjoys this macabre hobby and I keep her interested in it by feeding these plants chipped beef and bits of raw salt pork that they have the very devil digesting. I gave her American pitcher plant, which she calls Big Boy, a piece of pepperoni, and it has had its tongue hanging out for two weeks."

* * *

I see by the papers that it does no good to brush a dog's teeth or teach a dog, perhaps, to brush his own teeth. I have known this for a long while, but a lengthy study by a state university school of dentistry confirms it. Dogs were fed molasses and their teeth brushed with sugar to see if cavities could be induced, but not one cavity developed. At the end of the experiment all the dogs were released and romped back to their families saying, "Look, Ma, no cavities." Now the university is trying to discover what it is in a dog's mouth that resists carious lesions.

Well, this is an old story with me. Perhaps I didn't go about it scientifically, but I did brush a dog's teeth for the better of two years. I was a boy and the dog was a St. Bernard, and he used to eat two washtubfuls of food each week – a mixture of meat, vegetables and cornmeal.

He would also eat as much candy as anyone would feed him, as well as chocolate layer cake and saltwater taffy. He would work on three or four pieces of saltwater taffy most of an afternoon and occasionally insert a paw in his mouth to pry it away from his molars.

It occurred to me then that his teeth might do with brushing, but my family wouldn't buy a new toothbrush just for him, so I clandestinely used my father's toothbrush. My father would say to my mother: "Say, this is the strangest-smelling toothbrush. Have you been using it to scrub a salami or something?" And she would deny it and he would grumble on.

I can't say my St. Bernard was very happy having his teeth brushed every night at my bedtime. He would whimper and hide. He considered it an invasion of his privacy and he wanted no part of somebody else's toothbrush.

I was talking to The Bugle Lady's husband the other night about brushing dogs' teeth. As you know he is a dentist and a marvelous craftsman. When Digger, the Boxer, the neurotic dog in our neighborhood who carries a security blanket with him everywhere, why, when he lost some teeth biting an automobile fender, The Bugle Lady's husband made him a partial plate.

At first, when he barked his teeth would fly out and he would have to pick them up and trot home with them to have them reinserted. But dogs are naturally clever and Digger soon learned to bark with his mouth closed, a kind of muffled and very distinctive bark.

I think Digger may be the only dog in the world with a partial plate soaking in a tumbler of water beside him when he is sacked out in his dog house.

It was soon after he learned to bark with his mouth closed that Digger began to whistle. Now he is often called upon to entertain at neighborhood parties. He whistles the first five or six notes of "Home, Sweet Home" rather well, but after that you can't make head or tail out of *what* he is whistling.

I mean people are bored with him now and they say: "Look, I've heard him whistle "Home, Sweet Home," and unless he can whistle something else for once, tell him to knock it off." The feeling is that when you have heard one dog whistle, you've heard them all.

Life is tougher for Digger than for other dogs. Down at the corner hydrant Digger is not understood. I don't say he is rejected, although he thinks he is rejected, but the other dogs do regard him with astonishment when he shows up with his tattered security blanket and begins to whistle. I think dogs generally do not allow for much eccentricity among their kind.

Among the other talented dogs around here is the Dibbles' spaniel. He had been taught as a puppy to play a child's toy piano and he did pretty well as long as the piece was in the key of C without any sharps or flats. As he grew older he gave up his career at the piano and reverted to just plain dog, but the other dogs never let him forget his youthful arty airs.

He finally drifted away from his associates and disappeared forever into the oblivion that so often overtakes talented and piano-playing dogs. Now he just lies in the Dibbles' backyard and scratches his stomach and dreams of the dog he might have been.

I am afraid Digger's future is not much brighter. The world simply hasn't time for dogs who whistle.

CHAPTER X

Around the House

I have told you how Mrs. Peterson thumbs her nose at Fred, the mailman, when Fred has no mail to leave at her house. And I have said this lowers the property values here every time she does it. But now I must tell you about Green Eyes and dogs and our lawn. Green Eyes lowers the property values, too, and some of the neighbors are beginning to complain to me about it.

You see, Green Eyes stands by our front door and barks at dogs who come over to our front lawn. She began doing this about three weeks ago and it is terribly effective. There is a particularly aggressive dog with a most distinctive, insulting bark which lives in the next block, and Green Eyes has learned to imitate him beautifully. We have no idea what this dog says to other dogs when he barks, but other dogs react to him furiously, and they react the same way when Green Eyes imitates him.

The interesting thing is that when Green Eyes opens the front door and barks at dogs on our lawn they react first with astonishment, then with furious anger, and then with resignation. They finally leave and go to some other lawn and don't come back.

Whatever this bark conveys to a dog I don't know, but I suspect it is the most outrageous message possible. It was a neighbor who first called my attention to Green Eyes' barking.

I thought it was just another dog outside, but Mrs. McMurty saw me at the bus stop one evening and said: "How is your dear, sweet wife these days?" And I said; "Who wants to know?" (You get friendly with Mrs. McMurty and she takes advantage.) And she said: "I ask because I notice that she frequently comes to your front door and barks at dogs." And I said: "She runs her business her way and I run my business my way and I keep hoping my neighbors will do the same."

But I wondered about it and when I got home Green Eyes confessed all.

Now, a wife is not only a helpmeet but she is supposed to be a "love object." At least that's what all the books say. So I said to Green Eyes: "I really have no objection to your barking at dogs in our front yard because I have seen it is terribly effective. But, on the other hand, you are supposed to be a love object, and I believe it is difficult to regard as a love object a lady who is half Airedale."

And she said: "Oh, pooh. How long you going to be around town sailor? What ship you from?" And I said: "I'm sorry, but in memory I still hear you barking."

And she said: "Well, let's get something settled right now. What do you want more, love object or a flawless lawn?" And I said: "I know I am going to hate myself later for saying this, but, at the moment, a beautiful lawn is my choice. Once you have disposed of all the dogs in the neighborhood, there is plenty of time for you to recapture your old swinging self." And she said: "I have an idea I can handle both roles simultaneously." And that's where we left it.

So now the dogs go to the other side of the street when they pass our place and their lips curl and they show their teeth and their hackles rise. And the word down at the corner hydrant is to stay away from the Welch place.

I have never barked at dogs, but once I barked at a bear. It was in Yellowstone National Park, and I don't advise it. We were poor and were staying in a tent and using public facilities, and one night I conducted my little daughter, Marybeth, to the ladies' powder room. We passed a bear investigating a garbage can. I stopped about ten feet away from him and I barked and he looked at me. I barked again and he came slowly to me. I told Marybeth: "Stand perfectly still!" The bear sniffed my coat and suddenly raised a paw and pulled the whole side pocket out of my new sports jacket. He then went back to his garbage can and I have never barked at a bear since.

This experience has made me most cautious about barking at anything, and I don't doubt that if Green Eyes keeps at it, one of these days she'll find herself in a first-class dog fight, and I'll have to run out with a bucket of water to stop it.

Green Eyes is very fussy about the lawn and regards every weed as a mortal enemy and is careful that it gets proper nourishment and tender, loving care. Well, one day she came home with two gallons of liquid fish fertilizer and she said she had found a bargain. And I said: "Our lawn will smell like a shore dinner and every cat and dog in the neighborhood will be over here at once no matter how fiercely you bark."

And she said: "You're just making excuses so you won't have to put it on." And I said: "All right, I'll put it on. But with this hot weather and that stinking fish smell, a mob of neighbors will gather and they will burn down our house before the day is out." And she said: "If you soak it in with plenty of water, there won't be any odor."

Now, I really don't mind putting liquid fertilizer on the lawn because you just attach a bottle of it to the end of the hose and sprinkle it on mixed with water, and all the time I am doing it I can watch The Widow pulling weeds from her lawn while dressed in shorts and a tight top. So I started to put the fish fertilizer on at 3:45 P.M. and at 3:47 P.M. the first cat showed up. At 3:49 P.M. two more cats appeared, and at 4:00 P.M. I counted eight cats and five dogs and they were having a ball. The dogs were pushing themselves on their stomachs clear across the lawn, and the cats were rolling on their backs in it. I was watching The Widow.

Pretty soon my old friend Caesar, the big, friendly St. Bernard who lives down the street and always carries a barrel of martinis around his neck to rescue any of us lost travelers in the neighborhood, came along. I said: "Don't tell me that you are going to roll in this bargain basement stuff, too?" And he said: "It ain't likely, Doc. Us St. Bernards do not react to fish fertilizer like some of the lesser breeds. When I see lesser breeds reverting to ancestral practices, I am ashamed I am a dog."

Just then The Widow's lady poodle came along, the most stuck-up dog I ever saw, she expects you to take off your hat to her when you meet her on the street. And right down she went into the fertilizer and rolled in it, too. And Caesar said: "Just what I told you." The Widow came running and said: "Oh, Fifi, you naughty girl! What are you doing? Good heavens, Mr. Welch, what is that nasty stuff? It smells to high heaven."

And I said: "Any complaints should be made directly to the management, inside the house. My wife brings home bargains."

And The Widow said: "I just washed Fifi this morning so we could go out this evening, and here she is smelling like a fish fry."

And I said: "I would be delighted to wash your Fifi if you will assist, and if you would care to get down and roll a little, I would be delighted to wash you."

So we took Fifi around to the basement and pretty soon Green Eyes called down the basement stairs and asked: "What's going on down there?" And I said: "A couple of girls came over to play with me." And The Widow said: "It's me, Lola." and Fifi barked and Green Eyes came right down, and I explained: "Fifi rolled in that stinking stuff you gave me to put on the lawn."

It was Green Eyes' fault. She saved thirty cents a gallon and the whole neighborhood smelled like the tide was out. But did she take the blame? No. I finished washing Fifi and The Widow cleaned *me* up in a very sisterly way, but Green Eyes

HIS
McCAUSLAND

acted like I had sneaked a girl in from the other side of town. She said: "Oh, don't baby him, Lola. It's time he had his regular monthly shower, too."

So The Widow stayed for coffee and I took a bath, and the phone kept ringing. Others in the neighborhood had finally figured where their dogs and cats had picked up the aroma. And do you know what Green Eyes told them? She said: "I guess my husband put some fish fertilizer on the lawn." I did it all! But I think she will have to do a lot of barking now for a while to keep the dogs away, and I don't know what she will do about the cats.

* * *

For a time there Green Eyes and I were pretty good about calling the television stations and getting permission not to look at TV that evening when we had to go out for some important reason.

We had to clear it with only four channels, and I must admit that, on the whole, the stations were reasonable. I mean, I would call a station and say: "I was wondering if maybe instead of looking at teevee tonight it would be all right if my wife and I went for a walk?"

And they would say: "Walk *where?*" And I'd say: "Oh, just around the neighborhood. We like to walk around at night because people leave their shades up and you can look into their living rooms and kitchens and see how they furnish them. There is a good deal of depravity in our neighborhood, and you never know when you are going to catch a little of that, too."

Then the stations would say: "It will be all right this time, but don't let it happen too often."

Occasionally a station said: "We have a report here that you people have been reading books. We hope this is not true." And we would deny it because how can they check up?. You see, when we read books, we pull down all the shades and turn the television on loud and sneak into another room to read. Anyone outside the house would assume we were looking at television.

This is dangerous business because later, when they put you under oath and warn you about the dangers of perjury and ask you about the programs you pretended to see while reading, why, you could easily give yourself away. Fortunately, Grandma sits at the television constantly, switching from station to station so she will miss nothing, and she always gives us a summary at breakfast each morning so we can fake that we saw the shows ourselves.

Sometimes, though, she gets mixed up. She will be telling us about a show and will say: "And poor Mr. Hathaway had a terrible accident." And I will say: "Hold on, what part did he play?" And she will say: "He didn't have a part. It really happened. It's right there in the newspaper."

The morning this happened, the telephone rang and it was a survey and a voice said: "What program did you view last night?" And I said: "I caught the Hathaway Show where he was in a terrible accident, real exciting." And the voice said: "I thought it was a good show, too." Which proves to me that the voice was horsing around town the night before, itself. I say let the television companies purge their own ranks before they start purging the viewers.

* * *

Green Eyes reads all the dirty books for me. She thinks it is her duty to be a helpmeet and keep me up on modern literature and besides, she thinks the kindest thing she can do for me is to preserve whatever tiny bit of innocence I have preserved after a lifetime in the newspaper business.

But the other night she put down her book and said: "Our marriage is all wrong." And I said: "What did I do now?" And she said: "Oh, it isn't you. It's us. I've been reading all these best sellers and ours is just not a true American marriage." And I said: "What do you think we ought to do? I like it fine the way it is already." And she said: "All the husbands and wives in the best sellers have something going on the side. You never read about a husband or wife who is faithful."

And I said: "I've thought about it a lot, but the trouble is when I get done with work every day I am too tired to do anything but go straight home to dinner." And she said: "I know. You come home night after night on time. I never worry about where you are or whom you're with. And judging by the best sellers, which I assume reflect American married life as it *really* is today, you may be the only dependable husband in the whole country." And I said: "Thank you."

And she said: "I'm not sure you should thank me. Some people might consider it an indictment, or that you have no self-awareness." And I said: "I suppose I have opportunities. I meet pretty girls now and then at the office or downtown. But it stops there. I mean it takes so much *time* to wine and dine a girl and work up an affair. What time would I have left for my model railroad? Besides, when I talk to an attractive babe, my self-awareness always asks, 'Can she cook as well as you do?'"

And she said: "Maybe that's your trouble. All the men in these books having torrid love affairs never stop to eat. Perhaps you have built your life around food instead of sex. It is as much my fault as yours. I go through the whole day sometimes being happy in a perverted way while I am cooking up a fancy dish for your dinner without once thinking of losing myself in the enfolding arms of a handsome guy I picked up in a bar."

And I said: "Me, too. I tell myself I *must* think about sex the way the characters do in novels. I *must.* But a whole day goes by and I don't think about anything except the dry martini you are going to have waiting for me and what you're going to have for dinner."

And she said: "A lot of our friends seem to have marriages pretty much like ours, not like the novels. I suppose we can go on as we have, but we ought to keep it quiet. If we go on being compatible and in love with one another, the least we can do is pull down the curtains and not let anyone suspect. It is so terribly old-fashioned."

And I said: "I suppose if we put our minds to it, we could each work up some kind of an affair. But what bothers me is the late hours. Maybe, if we worked it right, we could knock off our affairs about 7:00 P.M. and both get home in time to have a nice, late dinner."

And she said: "That would mean I'd have to plan dinner and get the table set before I went off to my assignation. It would take all the careless spontaneity out of the affair. No chance for developing our self-awareness or exploiting our sexual potential with a variety of partners."

And I said: "It's a pretty bleak future. Nothing to look forward to but endless dull years of each other's love and companionship."

* * *

Green Eyes' mother is always seeking ways for me to make more money. Mostly it occurs to her when she sees me stretched out on the living room sofa with a newspaper over my face, trying to nap. She was brought up, I think, to believe that any time you see a man stretched out napping between dawn and sunset, why he could be better employed doing something gainfully.

So she comes in and reads to me. She reads Business Opportunities. Incidentally, I don't want to confuse my mother-in-law with Mr. Dibbles' mother-in-law who is eighty-five and smokes cigars and drinks brandy in bed, and stands on the front lawn in her bathrobe and waves at strangers in passing cars. My mother-in-law is sane and rational compared to Mr. Dibbles' mother-in-law. My mother-in-law, for instance, would like to bring a ton of manure into my nice clean basement and start growing mushrooms. She read to me from a magazine about how you Make Big Money from Mushrooms.

"Surprise and amaze your friends with your own private stock of fresh, home-grown mushrooms," my mother-in-law read, "Harvest your first crop in just thirty days!"

And I mumbled: "Look, I am trying to nap."

And she said: "Oh course, you would have to board up the basement windows. Cousin George could bring in a load or two of manure, and I don't think he would charge you anything for it. He is such a sweet person."

And I said: "Cousin George is a burglar, and if he brought us manure he would charge us twice what anybody else would have to pay."

And she said: "Well, lots of people are making Big Money growing mushrooms."

And I said: "How do you know they are?"

And she said: "It says so, right here."

And then she said: "I should think you could make a little extra money putting wren and bluebird houses together. Here is a place where they send you birdhouse kits. You glue the pieces together and paint cute sayings on them and sell the completed birdhouses to your neighbors."

And I said: "Sheesh!"

And she said: "Mr. William Lansing of South Bend, Indiana, spent only three evenings putting birdhouses together and selling them, and he made forty-five dollars the first week. Furthermore, he was Helping Bring the Bluebirds Back."

And I said: "I don't want to make money. I want to be a failure. And what is this about bringing the bluebird back? Where has he been?"

And she said: "It says here you have to write for particulars."

So I was just about asleep and she said: "There is Big Money in Fairy Whistles. They come from Yugoslavia, and the importer will give you Your Own Exclusive Territory if you

Act Now. They are gay, sunny-yellow, wooden whistles with finger holes so they can be played like flutes. Straight from Fairyland. They amuse the Young in Heart."

And I said: "I don't see me selling fairy whistles."

And she said: "The child blows the whistle and in his imagination there appears a real, live, beautiful fairy, with a crown and wand and dress and sparkling golden slippers."

And I said: "It would be my luck to try to sell a fairy whistle to somebody who wouldn't let me finish the whole sales pitch. I would say, 'Anybody here interested in a fairy whistle?' and they would punch me right in the nose."

And she said: "Here is a company that sends you genuine Algonquin moccasins and beads, and you put the beads on and sell them to your friends at a Big Markup."

And I called Green Eyes and said: "Honey, will you make your mother stop reading me this crud while I am trying to take a nap."

So now Green Eyes is sore at me and her mother is sore at me, and I am going to have to take both of them out to dinner because from the muttering out in the kitchen I know dinner here won't be fit to eat.

* * *

There used to be a week designated as National Thrift Week, but no more. Now even the President is telling us to spend and help cut inflation and encourage employment and Make the Economy Healthy by Spending. The trouble is, from earliest childhood I was taught to save, and now I can't kick the habit. A couple of times a month I walk into my bank with three or four dollars rolled up in my fist and I stand before the teller's cage in an agony of uncertainty. Then the teller finally comes around from behind the cage and prys the money away from me and deposits it in my name before I can change my mind. It is a new underground service the bank offers called enforced savings. They have to offer it or they won't have enough cash to loan at high interest rates.

So then I don't have enough money for lunch that day and have to borrow a couple of dollars from the branch manager. The trouble is that Green Eyes handles all our money and looks after deposits and balancing accounts and like that and gives me only ten dollars a week for pocket money. I can charge my meals where I ordinarily eat, but suppose I have a business engagement with some glamorous woman and want to eat at a different place where I don't have to share her with my usual boisterous male companions? It is all right on Monday when I have a whole ten dollars to waste on riotous living. But along about Friday I have only ninety cents or so, and it is embarrassing to have a glamorous woman business acquaintance rummaging in her bag for the difference when she assumed she was my guest. She might think I'm tight or something.

I believe I am the only man in town who gets money *from* headwaiters and waiters. I know two places where the headwaiter slips me a fiver when he is seating me at the table, and there must be seven or eight places where the waiter always leaves me a dollar or two under my plate. Of course it all depends on the kind of service I give him. It is more, I find, when I brush off the crumbs with my own napkin and when I stack the dishes for him on the table. If I ignore him, it is less, and sometimes nothing.

All that the waiters and headwaiters who tip me ask in return is that I eat quickly and leave so they can turn the table over to someone who is more lively. On two occasions, also, hat-check girls have furtively plunged a ten or twenty into my breast pocket and whispered: "Here, get yourself a new hat."

I have told this to Green Eyes many times, but, the truth is, she doesn't believe me. She makes out our income tax return and brings it to me to sign, but she won't let me see it. I wonder if I went to the Internal Revenue people whether they would let me see my return. When I get only ten dollars a week, I shouldn't think I would have to pay any tax at all.

* * *

There is nothing like having a singing woman around the house. When you hear your wife singing it is a sign maybe everything is going better than you thought. Maybe she's happy. Maybe she's pleased with you. A fellow can sit back and relax a little.

Of course when my mother-in-law sings, that's a different thing. Like I told you, Grandma is in her 80s and a dear lady, but she firmly believes that Men Are Beasts and should be Kept In Their Place, and when she sings she belts out numbers like "My Man Done Did Me Wrong" and "Oh, You Nasty Man, You" and "I Wish You Were Dead, You Rascal You," and like that.

Green Eyes sings mostly when the grandchildren are visiting. It takes their minds off their food. Very small children never seem hungry. I don't believe they eat from one week to another. I have never seen the young ones voluntarily eat. But when Green Eyes sings to them they are distracted and scarcely seem aware that she is stuffing them like a sausage.

Just this noon Green Eyes was singing to our two youngest grandchildren, Dougie II and Mimi. She was singing about a couple of creeps who threw a kitty-cat down a well. It was more complicated than that. One kid, a certain Tommy Green, threw the cat down the well. He was the Bad Guy. And another kid, Johnny Stout, pulled the cat out. He was the Good Guy.

I don't suppose Mimi got much out of it. She liked the tune and smiled widely, showing a lot of mashed potato. But you could see the message was getting to Dougie II. It was obvious to me that he was trying to make up his mind whether he wanted to be a Bad Guy and throw pussy cats down wells, or be a Good Guy and pull them out. Or maybe, successively, be *both*.

And I said to Green Eyes: "I do not believe you should be singing to my grandchildren about disturbed, hostile kids throwing cats down wells." And she said: "Oh, pooh! It's only a nursery rhyme and it never hurt anybody."

Then she sang to them about a precocious kid named Georgie Porgie who got his kicks kissing girls and making them cry, and an exhibitionist named Wee Willie Winkie who ran around town in his nightgown, upstairs and downstairs, rapping at windows and crying through locks. A regular monster, scaring other kids to death. I suppose he felt rejected because he was undersize and was called "Wee Willie" and had a grudge against society.

I have very serious doubts about whether my grandchildren should be hearing things like this. I know I, myself, have scarcely been able to face an egg since I first heard about Humpty Dumpty.

* * *

I find it difficult to concentrate. The smallest noise bothers me when I am writing at home. There is a lady up the block, for instance, who calls her kid. He hides. From my second-story window I can see him crouching in the alley. I know from bitter experience that his mother will call endlessly until he answers. She has a voice that pierces metal and shatters water glasses.

It is a funny thing. When you meet her dressed up at a party she is gorgeous, feminine and soft-spoken. Butter wouldn't melt in her mouth. She has kind of a husky voice and men go out of their minds. She works part time for a realtor and I think she could sell igloos in the Bahamas without a bit of effort. But when she hollers for her kid she becomes primitive.

So I go to the window and shout down at the kid: "Your mother is calling you, you little beggar. Why don't you answer?" And he says things like: "Oh, shut up! and "Who asked you?" My own voice won't carry to his mother so I have to phone her. "Your kid is down here hiding behind a garbage can in the alley," I tell her, and she gives me that sultry routine and it's like a go-pill. But a minute later she is back at her door screaming like a monster. A dual personality for sure.

Green Eyes never screamed for our children. She used to have a doorman's whistle. She gave it one long blast and that was it. It was a three-note chime and it was pleasant to hear. Of course there were disadvantages, too. Occasionally a cruising taxi cab would stop at our house expectantly.

I wish I could concentrate and ignore distractions like the great Russian composer Glinka. His memoirs tell us that "he could sit in his parlor with a flock of pet birds flying around his head and with three or four friends talking and carousing at his elbow, and calmly write his "Kamarinskaya."

I must try writing with birds flying around my head some day. Then Green Eyes would say to a visitor: "Douglass is in his study writing. You can talk to him through the door, but don't open it. All his birds will fly out." She is tidy. And I doubt that she would agree to allowing my friends in to carouse. In fact I know she wouldn't.

A British psychiatrist says that when you are distracted nothing restores peace of mind and the ability to concentrate like turning on the television to an empty channel and imagining your own program. You are director, writer and actors or actresses, and you play out your fantasies.

I tried it and Green Eyes spoiled it all. She came into the room and saw me sitting at the television tuned to an empty channel, and she said: "What are you doon, for heaven sake?" And I said; "I am escaping for a while so I can concentrate. I am projecting fantasies onto that screen." And she said: "What are you playing at the moment?" And I said: "I am dancing in Old Vienna and the band is playing a graceful waltz, and all the world smiles on me tonight." And she said: "I can just see you, tall, straight and handsome in your Hussar's uniform." And I said: "No. I am wearing a dress, very bouffant, and it rustles as I twirl."

And she promptly turned off the TV and said: "Iron pills, that's what you need. Iron pills, lots of iron." I don't know why she should seem so disturbed, do you?